He knelt for a moment beside he
looking down at her, thin
young and vulnerab
that moment
from sel
riding to
he'd been

Then he th
himself for
many years for a few
minutes of lus a girl with a
baby face who'd picked the wrong
man to marry. His own peace of
mind wasn't worth it.

'Please, darling Jed.'

She smiled up at him . . .

Also in this series

HERNE THE HUNTER 1: WHITE DEATH
HERNE THE HUNTER 2: RIVER OF BLOOD
HERNE THE HUNTER 3: THE BLACK WIDOW
HERNE THE HUNTER 4: SHADOW OF THE VULTURE

and published by Corgi Books

John J. McLaglen

Herne the Hunter
5: Apache Squaw

CORGI BOOKS
A DIVISION OF TRANSWORLD PUBLISHERS LTD

HERNE THE HUNTER 5: APACHE SQUAW

A CORGI BOOK 0 552 10526 0

First publication in Great Britain

PRINTING HISTORY
Corgi edition published 1977

This book is set in 10 on 12 pt. Intertype Baskerville

Corgi Books are published by
Transworld Publishers Ltd.,
Century House, 61–63 Uxbridge Road,
Ealing, London W5 5SA
Made and printed in Great Britain by
Cox & Wyman Ltd., London, Reading and Fakenham

This is for Elizabeth, with my continuing love and thanks. I still get drunk out of my mind, merely from the fact that you are here.

Chapter One

The thin cotton of her pale blue shirt chafed at her nipples, making them tender and painful. Emmie-Lou switched the reins from right hand to left, rubbing at her breasts, conscious of the continuous trickle of sweat that ran between them. Shifting in the saddle to ease the discomfort from moist thighs. Wishing that Elisha wasn't such an old-fashioned husband, and would let her ride astride in trousers, like some of the other women around the ranch.

'Want a break, Mrs. Parsons?'

She wished that the ramrod, Peter Tanner, wouldn't put that leer into everything he said. Pete could even make a request for a second helping of beans sound like something downright immoral. But he'd been with her husband, Elisha, for the best part of twenty years. In lots of ways Pete was closer to Elisha than she was. When they rode out west from Virginia, both wild boys from the mountains, looking for land and money, she hadn't even been a gleam in her Pappy's eye.

Now she was eighteen, and Lishe was near forty, with the ways of a man a full twenty years more. Although the temperature was over the hundred, the sun baking the dusty land, Emmie-Lou shuddered.

'I asked you if'n you wanted to take a little break, Mrs. Parsons. Maybe have a lie down and take some of the weight off'n your . . .'

Tanner left the sentence dangling, turning his head away with a gap-toothed grin, spitting a dirty stream of tobacco juice at a towering saguaro cactus alongside the narrow trail.

Emmie-Lou brushed red sand from her black skirt, a short quirt dangling from her right wrist, wishing that she could raise the whip and lash the ramrod across his sneering face. But she knew that Tanner would tell her husband, and Lishe wouldn't take kindly to such behaviour towards an old friend like Pete.

'No. I guess I'm happy to ride on a while.'

'Yes sir, Mrs. Parsons. You're the boss, ma'am. Sure as heck are. Damned if your word ain't good enough for old Pete. I'll go along with anything you like. *Anything* at all.'

She breathed deep, trying to clear away the touch of his presence at her shoulder. Ever since she'd gone out for a ride away from the echoing mansion in the middle of nowhere, only three weeks after the wedding, and just kept on riding, Lishe had always made sure that there was a man with her. And that man had to be someone that her husband trusted not to be tricked or bribed by Emmie-Lou. And that man was always Pete Tanner.

'You see that?'

There was an unusually sharp note to Tanner's voice, and the girl looked round, shaking the long black hair off her face, wiping sweat from her cheeks with the back of one gloved hand. Staring to where his hand pointed. Up and away to the left, where several deep arroyos snaked down from the foothills of the Mogollons, their depths in shadow as the sun slanted across them.

'I don't see nothing.'

'Thought I saw a man. Maybe not. Can't tell this far off. Guess we might make a turn for home now, Mrs. Parsons.'

It was an order and not a polite suggestion, and they both knew it. But these rides out, once every other month, were the only contact the girl had with reality, away from the cold marble blackness of the great house, set in the middle of one of the biggest spreads in the whole of the South-West. The land that had made Elisha Parsons one of the richest men in the Territory of New Mexico. Riches that had set the barefoot boy from Virginia to thinking about a son and an heir.

And a wife.

Strictly in that order of importance.

A wind sprang up from out of nowhere, setting the dust-devils whirling, and the horses skittering sideways.

'God damn it to Hell!' spat Tanner, kicking his heels into his roan's flanks, drawing blood with the Mexican rowels. 'Still, you son-of-a-bitch bastard!'

'Lishe wouldn't take kindly to hearing that you'd used that kind of language in front of me, Tanner,' said Emmie-Lou, glad to have the opportunity to put down the ramrod for once. Knowing that Tanner feared her husband as much as anyone, despite their long-standing friendship.

'Yeah, well ...' he grunted, finally bringing the horse under control. 'I guess that you wouldn't be the one to tell him, would you, Mrs. Parsons? Not if'n I was to say that I figured you was gettin' ready to go a'runnin' again. I guess that old Lishe wouldn't take none too kind to that neither.'

'That'd be a lie!'

'Might be a lie to say you done it. Wouldn't be a lie to say you was thinkin' 'bout it. I watch you, and I know what you think most your wakin' moments. I see your eyes go to those hills, and there ain't no help comin' from them. You married him, and you are surely married to him until the day you die.'

Emmie-Lou wiped sticky dust from her face and stood in the stirrups, feeling the hot leather of the saddle peeling from the sweaty skin on the inside of her thighs. The trouble was, Tanner was right. All the way along the line and then clear back again. She knew it. He knew it. And he knew that she knew. There just wasn't a way around it.

The marriage had started off as a terrible mistake and got worse from there. Elisha Parsons had come courting to Magdalena. Her home town in the towering shadow of South Baldy Mountain, one hundred and fifty miles north and east of his spread. Brought there by the word of the prettiness of Widow Harvey's daughter. And he'd found they'd told the truth. Some cow-towns and they'd call a girl pretty who wasn't crippled or downright ugly. But Magdalena hadn't got a finer sight than Emmie-Lou Harvey swinging down to church, in her best bonnet and dress, her black hair tied demurely back, and blue eyes staring at her feet.

Pete Tanner remembered it well, the day that Lishe came back from his courting. 'She's a sweet little sixteen, Pete,' his boss had said. 'You know the sort I mean. And I'm aiming to have her for the mother of my sons.'

Tanner had told that to Emmie-Lou. Lots of times. Just to make sure she didn't get too damned uppity with him. That had been two years back. And in those two years there hadn't been no sign of a son. Nothing to show at all. And God knows but Elisha had tried. Labouring over her like she was a brood mare, which she was. Every night the same.

Coming three parts drunk up the echoing stairs, with the banisters of mahogany, imported clear from France in Europe. Lurching along the dim corridors, lined with expensive oil-paintings of fat ladies sporting among water meadows with pink cherubs. Tripping over the fragile furniture with spindly legs that he claimed had cost as much as a whole year's cattle drive.

Into the bedroom, with its monster canopied four-poster, made from English oak, carved with animals of kinds that Emmie-Lou had never seen before. A sort of horse with a great single horn from its brow and something that resembled a shaggy cougar.

Shaking the hair away from her face, Emmie-Lou

thought back to the nights in the house, and suddenly felt cold in the heat of the New Mexico sunlight.

Lishe was a hard man. Had to be to build up a spread that size, and hold it against the marauding Chiricahua and Mescalero Apaches. And against the Mex bandits that came silently from south of the big river, risking being caught by the U.S. Cavalry on their way over, and by the federales on their way back with women or cattle or American dollars.

Every now and again, when the day was going well, and his stomach was lined with a slick coating of cheap whiskey, Pete Tanner would open up to the girl on their rides, and talk about the good old days. The days when he and Lishe were boys among the blue-tipped mountains back home, with the sun on their backs and no cares to weigh them down. It was hard for the girl to equate that talk with the stony face of the man she had married.

When he came courting her, Elisha Parsons had smiled some. Told her all about the spread he owned. The house he'd built. The family he was looking to raise. And she was very young and Magdalena hadn't got any man like Elisha. With his toughness and confidence. Her mother was impressed, and a little bit jealous, as mothers always will be when their only daughter gets married.

The difference between their ages didn't seem so bad. Not so bad then, two years back. Now it seemed a great empty gulf that lay between them, and Emmie-Lou knew in her heart that she would never be able to cross that immeasurable depth.

'Don't like all this damned dust, Mrs. Parsons. Blowin' round like this, might be hidin' half a hundred Mex bastards, or half the Apache nation.'

Tanner's voice tugged her back to the present, and Emmie-Lou looked around them. The mountains rose about like peaks of flame, and the way back lay through Pinnacle Canyon, with its steep sides and boulder-strewn deeps. For a moment she shared the older man's concern, then she wondered if an attack by bandits or Indians might not give her the chance to slip away once more. Despite Lishe's awful threat of what he would do to her if she ever ran from him again.

Racing in on the heels of that thought came the one that said it maybe wouldn't be that bad even if she did get taken prisoner. Not by the filthy Apaches, though there was an odd thrill of excitement at the idea of being possessed by an imperious, naked savage, but by a romantic bandit with a gleaming moustache and a sombrero with a fringe of golden coins, taking her across the pommel of his white stallion to his hacienda among the hills below the Rio Grande.

It would be different from Elisha's panting brutality.

'Set your spurs in! I don't like this one bit. Heard from one of them dog-face soldier boys at the Fort that there was trouble on one of the rancherias way west. Handful of bucks set to raise Hell and win a name. Come on, Ma'am!'

Tanner kicked his horse up to a full gallop, and Emmie-Lou followed him, rapping her horse in the flanks with the heels of her boots, pushing it on towards the pass and the safety of home.

They were round about fifteen miles from the house, cut off from it by a spur of the Mogollons, its lower slopes dappled with white-tipped spears of yucca, growing in sparse clumps. Any one of them big enough to hold a half dozen Mescaleros. Wisps of cloud were gathering to the west.

The pillar of dust about them was whipped up by the wind, and Emmie-Lou, riding on behind the clattering hooves of Tanner's mount, couldn't see more than a few paces in front of her. She was conscious of the pounding in her own heart from the excitement. Wondering if the isolated routine of her miserable life would be altered by today.

There was even the unbidden thought creeping out of one of the locked rooms at the back of her mind that if there were really Apaches loose in the area and looking for blood, then maybe they'd already have attacked the ranch. Maybe Elisha was already dead. Maybe she was free and didn't know it.

The girl opened her mouth and laughed, spitting out the red sand over her shoulder. Tanner heard the noise and peered back, unable to believe the sound of laughter from Lishe's wife. Deciding it must have been a cough and riding on.

The saddle between her thighs was wide and firm, and she closed and opened her muscular legs on it, feeling the warmth and excitement flood through her with the rhythmic pounding across the trail. Nearer and nearer to Pinnacle Canyon. Feeling her nipples hardening against her shirt as she lay forward over her horse's neck. Managing to forget her husband's crude and indifferent love-making. Though love was a word that didn't seem to exist in Lishe's mind. Nor affection. Nothing but cold, fierce anger in his own possession.

'You leave me and I'll find you, even if you hide under the stones of Hades. And I'll bring you back, like I got you back last time. And this time I'll make sure that you never run nowhere again. You hear me, wife?'

'Yes.'

'I married you for a child. A son. And when you've given me that, then you can go where you like. Sink to the filthy whorin' level I raised you from. Rolling in the dust and baring your belly to the sun for all I care. But first there's my son you owe me.'

It was a heavy debt. And despite all Lishe's panting and pounding, nothing happened. Month followed month and nothing happened that didn't always happen to her.

They were only a couple of hundred yards from the gaping mouth of the deep arroyo, Tanner easing back to make sure the woman stayed with him. He knew what good old Lishe had promised her if she got away from him, and he knew him well enough and long enough to be certain that their friendship wouldn't save him from Lishe's anger if he let Emmie-Lou escape while out with him.

'Ease up now. Ease up!'

Emmie-Lou tugged the reins, forcing her lathered horse from a gallop to a loping trot, blinking through the dust to see Tanner's back. It had been close by Pinnacle Canyon that the Apaches had come whooping out of the sun eight years back, hitting the wagons bringing provisions to the spread. Killing three men and taking a woman with them. The soldiers had ridden out and burned down a small camp, sabring an old woman and six little toddlers. But they never found any of the food and ammunition that the Mescaleros had taken.

Nor the woman.

'Seems quiet enough. I'm going first, and you come after me. About fifty paces behind. And if you got any of your clever ideas 'bout goin' . . .?'

'I'll be right behind you, Tanner.'

He spat again, the stream of brown splattering into the dust close by her horse's front hooves. 'That's real good. I'll be able to to tell Lishe how good you been today. Please him, that will.'

He looked away from her, letting his gaze roam up and around the sheer walls, to the stark line of the top of the arroyo. Their own trail had settled as they sat, and Emmie-Lou could see clear behind them for thirty or forty miles. Thirty or forty miles of shimmering nothingness. Just a few spindly saguaro cactuses breaking the horizon, like sentinels pointing the way to the sky.

A thousand feet above the heads of the waiting couple, a buzzard circled patiently on a thermal of hot air, bounced back from the oven of rock. It had been watching the vast area of desert beneath it with idle interest, seeking the clues that would mean food. The two people riding fast on horseback had been ignored. But now they sat still and quiet. Only the tails of the mounts flicking out. Perhaps they might be worth watching for a while. Effortlessly, the big bird let its right wing drop a fraction and it began a long swirling descent.

'You're getting to be a frightened old man, Tanner,' sneered the girl, standing in the stirrups, gazing around the mouth of the canyon, and up to where the bright sun etched the top of the narrow pass. Not a thing stirred. Not a sound.

'I seen bodies after the Indians finished with 'em. Gives a man an idea about what fear means. Don't mean being scared of dark. Means being frightened of being hurt. I been lucky, 'part from a few breaks and losin' my teeth to a damned quack in Albuquerque. But those bodies . . .'

Emmie-Lou had seen something of them, before Lishe had ordered her in. Seen the faces that didn't have anything that would make them faces. Eyes, nose, lips and teeth. Ears. All gone. And the fingers and the toes and the hands and the feet. And . . .

And everything else.

She had run to her room and been sick, bringing up all that she'd eaten and drunk that day. Retching until there was only bitter bile. For the first time, Emmie-Lou began to feel the fear coming from Tanner.

'Come on. Slow and easy.'

The ramrod heeled his mount forwards, the hooves pattering in the soft sand, heading out of the blazing sun into the cool shadows of the arroyo. Emmie-Lou waited until he was fifty paces ahead of her, and then moved on. Seeing him half-turn his head to make sure she was following.

The sides of Pinnacle Canyon opened wider for the first eighty yards, then corkscrewed and closed in, until it seemed as if a rider could reach out and touch both walls at the same time. The girl kept her distance, taking deep breaths, trying to keep calm. Telling herself that Tanner hadn't been *sure* that he'd seen anything. That the dust-devils might have been just that. And nobody had actually *seen* any parties of bucks off their land. The Cavalry had scouts out patrolling the whole time, so it surely wasn't going to be possible for Apaches to get this close to their spread without someone noticing.

She had succeeded in convincing herself that there was nothing to be frightened of before she even reached the part of the arroyo where it narrowed right down.

'Close up, Mrs. Parsons,' said Tanner, just out of sight around the first sharp corner.

Away from the direct light and heat of the banking sun, Emmie-Lou felt chilled and reached up to button her open shirt. Looking down to concentrate on what she was doing, letting the horse walk forwards at its own pace.

She never saw or heard the Apaches on their unshod ponies as they rode in alongside her, moving up from behind. The first she knew was when a hand touched her on the arm, with a gentleness that was somehow more shocking than an explosion of violence.

Although she tried to cry out, her throat had closed up in panic, and only a barely audible gasp came out. There were two of them, she saw at first, but she could make out more riding in behind. Small men, in cotton blouses and trousers, wearing soft leather boots. Headbands of various colours holding back their shoulder-length hair.

Emmie-Lou closed her eyes for a second, wondering if she would faint. Still not a sound had been made, and there came a moment of wild hope. Hope that they hadn't seen Tanner, and that the resourceful man might find a way of rescuing her.

The boom of the rifle from ahead, and the cry of pain that followed, killed that hope. The voice had been that of the ramrod. Which meant that she was on her own. The Indian on her right had been watching her face and he laughed, the noise startling in the echoing arroyo, completing the fright for the buzzard, which had gone skittering aloft again at the crash of the gun.

'Now you close up, Mrs. Parsons,' he mocked, in hoarse but good English.

As they rode on, around the bend, Emmie-Lou Parsons felt the thin cotton of her pale blue shirt chafing at her nipples, making them tender and painful.

She wondered what Elisha would think.

Chapter Two

'Get up!'

'No.'

'I said to get up and face me!'

'I said "No" and that's what I meant.'

'You're a coward!'

'Go home, son.'

'A coward. A stinkin' lousy yellow-bellied coward! That's what you are.'

'If I stand up, then I'm going to have to fight you, son. I don't stand up for nothing, and that means I'll have to draw against you.'

'That's what I want, you bastard!'

'And then I'll kill you.'

It was a long, long silence, that dragged on in the small saloon. The older man at the table, his long black hair greying at the temples, took another pull at the long glass in front of him, looking as cool as a rich widow at a church social.

'You . . . you can't know that.'

The confidence had gone from the boy's voice, standing five paces in front of the table, fingers twitching nervously over the polished butts of a fine pair of matched forty-five Colts. He was tall and skinny, swallowing hard and making his Adam's Apple leap in his throat like a rabbit in a bag. His clothes were expensive, hanging well on his lean frame. A man in the corner shifted uncomfortably in his chair, making it scrape on the sawdust covered floor.

'Don't . . .' warned the boy, spinning round, half-drawing the right-hand gun.

'You only goin' to draw that one, then why weight yourself down with the other?'

'Listen, Mister . . . Herne. I know all about your reputation, and it don't mean more to me than a streak of chicken-shit on a wall. It's too long ago, and you ain't done nothing and killed nobody in years. So just come on outside and let's see if you're still what they say you was once if you was what they say you might . . .'

'Kind of lost your way in that mass of words, didn't you, son?' said the man at the table, casually pouring himself another shot from the bottle at his elbow. But his eyes never left the boy's face, and he poured left-handed, his right hand staying close to the worn butt of his own Colt. Jed Herne had been around too long and lost too many friends to take any sort of challenge lightly.

'I'll kill you where you sit, you bastard!'

'Talk a good fight, son. I'll credit you with that. Not a lot of sense, but a load of lip.'

Two hectic spots of red burned high on the young man's cheeks, and his mouth opened and shut convulsively. Herne looked at him sympathetically. Ever since the death of his own young wife, and the vengeance trail that he had ridden*

(**See earlier volumes in the Herne series, also available from Corgi.*)

word had spread like a brush fire through the South-West that Herne the Hunter was back.

Jed Herne had been one of the deadliest of the set of killer gunmen that dominated that part of the country through the eighteen-sixties up to then, along with Hardin, Hickok, Josiah Hedges, Garrett and the others. Names painted in blood and feared everywhere. Then Herne the Hunter had vanished. Some said killed. Those few who knew said he was married. But it was one target less for the young punks across the frontier who still wanted to win a name for themselves.

Then he'd come back. Back on the streets, looking for money to eat and to pay for his bullets. And to pay for the European education of Becky Yates. Daughter of his neighbour whose wife had died in the same savage incident as Jed's own beloved Louise. To remove her from the threat of death, and to keep her out of his hair and off his mind, Jed had sent her to a school in England. She'd been there for several months now, and he hoped would be there for another three years or so. Until 1885, when she would be coming on eighteen, and maybe capable of looking after herself.

Now he was down in New Mexico, fresh off the stage in Lordsburg. Looking for action. And finding the wrong kind in this glory-hunting kid. Trying to avoid killing the boy.

Who had finally fought himself and his nerves and was still standing near the table. Voice under control, fingers still close to the guns.

'Mister Herne, I want you to do me a favour.'

'Surely. All you have to do is ask.'

Out of the corner of his eye, Jed saw a tall man in worn trail clothes changing seats to bring him more directly behind where he was sitting. Herne held up his left hand to interrupt the boy.

'Wait on a moment there. The fellow in the grey stetson

carrying the single-action Wesson rimfire. Like to see him, with his hands well above the table, find a seat away from my back. Like an itch I can't see to scratch where he's just moved.'

Nothing happened, and he readied himself for instant action, suspecting he'd been tricked to a double set-up, with the kid as the decoy.

'Some folks go for countin'. I don't. I just say for someone to move, and if'n they don't, I have to reason they're not special friendly to me, and I kill them.'

As he snapped out the last word, he spun round in the chair, coming to his feet in a fluid blur of movement, his gun appearing in his fist, ready cocked, pointing at the man in the stetson.

Whose hand hovered in the fatal no-man's land between hip and holster. Eyes opened wide in panic and shock, set in a face that was white as paper.

'Mister . . . don't . . . please . . . I . . .'

'Put your gun up, Mister Herne.'

Without moving a muscle of his body, keeping the gaping barrel of the Colt steady on the man's throat, Herne answered the boy. 'You give me a reason, boy. And make it a good one.'

'He's my Uncle. Brother of my Ma. She got to hear what I was planning to do, and I guess he was here to try and back-shoot you to save me.'

There was a deadly bitterness in the boy's voice, and he looked away. The other man nodded quickly, and then realizing that was like an admission of murder, shook it again.

'Wouldn't have tried to kill you or nothing, Mister Herne. Aimed to wing you and save the boy.'

'Out. Go on. Out! And don't try that kind of damned stupid trick ever again. Or you won't live to be buried looking neat and tidy.'

Never looking at his nephew, the man scuttled across the

saloon, his boot-heels the only noise in the silence, through the bat-wing doors, that clattered for a moment or two after he'd gone.

Only then did Herne glance round at the boy, keeping the gun in his hand. Cocked and ready. 'You reckon I'm going to be needing this, son?' he asked, his voice calm and kindly.

'No.' Barely audible. Then louder. 'No. You won't be needing to use that, Mister Herne, and . . .'

Sensing the apology on the way, and not wanting it, Jed grinned, looking suddenly younger, and eased back the hammer of the Colt with his thumb, swinging it into the smooth holster with a gesture that he had used thousands of times.

'Share this gut-rotting stuff, or your Ma have words about that as well?'

The tension had gone, and Herne could relax, letting the tight spring inside himself uncoil. Knowing from experience that the moment had been and gone. The boy would not now face him. Although he had nothing but contempt for the Uncle that let the lad face the gunman while he sneaked around to blast a hole in his back, he had helped him in a way. By giving him a chance to show his class and speed, which he knew would be infinitely superior to anything the boy could ever have seen before.

'I'll have a glass, if I might, Mister Herne. And I'm real sorry about . . .'

'Friend of mine back in the Cavalry, named Nath Brittles used to say: "Never apologize. It's a sign of weakness." Not saying he was all right, but better than part-way.'

'Sure. But, you were just . . . amazing. I've never seen that kind of speed. I practice and practice. My finger wore clean through across the palm here, and the thumb, and the first finger. But I'll never . . .'

'That's right, son. Guess you'll never. I been around a long times, and I don't see a lot of boys up and coming all festy and ready to take me. Life's too easy, son.'

The first glass slipped down easy as winking, while the saloon gradually returned to normal. Bottles chinking, and talk whispering back from the corners. Lordsburg hadn't seen anything like it since Ringo had stepped down from the stagecoach with his guns blazing. Men were hurrying out, and returning, with more in tow, all wanting to take a look at Herne the Hunter, and tell each other the story of his speed over and over again.

But all that was stale to Jed, and he ignored it, concentrating on the boy. He'd already saved his life by not meeting him out in the street. Now he was trying to save him from himself.

'But you must have started somewheres, Mister Herne. By practicing.'

'That's the difference between you and me, boy. By the way, what's your name? Might have killed you and never known your name.'

'That would have been something for you, wouldn't it?' asked the boy intrigued at the idea.

'Guess so,' replied Herne, not wanting to tell him that he'd killed more nameless men than the boy had seen summers.

'I'm called Billy. Billy Joe Stewart.'

Solemnly, Jed reached across the table and shook the boy's hand. 'I'm honoured to make your acquaintance, Billy Joe.'

'Likewise, Mister Herne. And like I say, I'm powerful sorry about . . .'

Jed waved a cautioning finger. 'Sign of weakness, you recall. Sign of weakness.'

Billy Joe blushed, and let his fingers play with each other across the table, to cover his embarrassment, like two pink crabs in a rock-pool. 'You was goin' to tell me about how you began as a gunman, Mister Herne. The way you got so fast.'

'I didn't practice much early on, boy. I guess you'd be about . . . eighteen or so, and spent most your life here in Lordsburg?'

'I'm eighteen in three months. And I been to the west coast once with my Pa, before he passed on.'

'I was just fifteen when I rode the Pony Express with crazy Billy Cody. Twenty-three long years ago. Seems like it happened a hundred years back. Time I was your age I'd ridden a thousand miles with Quantrill in the War. Before my twentieth birthday, Billy Joe, I'd killed more men than I care to recall and was faster with a hand-gun than you'll ever be. Indians. Mexicans. Feds. Officers. Some women. Maybe even some children. Times I'd lie awake in those hours when sleep wouldn't come a'callin' on me, and I'd try to recall some of them. And they all sort of faded.'

Unconsciously, his voice had risen with the recalled pain, and the saloon was silent again, everyone listening as a legend sat in front of them and told them how it was.

'I could remember . . . sort of parts . . . like a face here, with a mouth open. Maybe the way one man was shot through the eye. Or an Indian . . . Cheyenne, say . . . or an Arapaho . . . falling with my bullet in his gut, screaming in his own tongue. Jesus Christ, Billy Joe! There was so much damned pain and death I can't remember it. Won't remember it. If I recalled a part of it, then I'd go out back of this filthy flop-joint and I'd take this Colt from its holster. Put the muzzle in my mouth and put a bullet through my brain.'

The last few sentences were almost shouted by the gunman, and he sat back, reaching for the bottle with fingers that weren't shaking. Not so much you'd notice.

Dropping his voice. 'That's why I'm fast, boy. That's why I could kill you and ride on and never look back or ever think of you again.'

The boy sat and looked at the older man. Round about the

age that his Pa might have been if it hadn't been for the fever back in sixty-nine.

Jed stared across at him, and half-laughed. 'Guess I sounded off a mite there, Billy Joe.'

'I'll never forget it. Never. Not a word, Mister Herne. And I'm . . .'

'Not sorry.'

Billy Joe grinned, wiping the palms of his hands across his trousers, wondering why he was sweating so much. 'No. Not sorry. I'm . . . thankful to you.'

As Jed looked round the saloon, the conversation sprang self-consciously back to life. He leaned across the table, letting his voice fall so that it carried no further than the ears of Billy Joe Stewart.

'You been lucky tonight, son. Most times the lesson you seen here would have been paid for you by you lying on your back in this place, with your eyes sort of misting over and cold running out of your stomach. You've had it easy. So stay lucky. Go home, Billy Joe. Stay home. Marry a good woman. Here in Lordsburg. Or anyplace. It don't give a sweet damn where. Raise your kids and die of old age day after your hundredth birthday. And never forget the night back in eight-two you near died. No, don't you tell me anything. Just go and good luck.'

'Thanks.' Still the boy hesitated, wondering whether to shake hands or what.

Herne settled it for him with a casual wave of the hand. '*Vaya con dios*, Billy Joe.'

The young boy nodded, and walked from the saloon, the guns still swinging from the hip, steeling himself not to look back. Herne grinned, and waved a hand to call for another bottle, which arrived at his table at the same moment as a hard-faced man in his forties. The stranger sat down without a word, and pulled out a picture of a woman. Beautiful, with a mane of black hair.

Helped himself to a drink from the bottle, still without a word, and leaned back, eyes on Herne, watching while he studied the picture.

'Pretty.'

No answer.

'You selling or buying, Mister?'

'Take care.'

'No. You take care. If you're selling, then thanks a lot but no thanks. If you want to buy, then you start asking the right way or get off your ass and out of here.'

'Nobody speaks to me like that.' The voice was still cold and quiet. Like a reptile skin sliding over smooth ice. But there was a tightening of the skin round the eyes.

'I do. Either piss or move away from the bucket. It's not a game.'

'Very well. You are Jedediah Herne.'

'That's not a question. You know it.'

'I do. I want you to find this woman and bring her back to my home.'

The obvious question was who she was.

'How much?'

'Two thousand five hundred dollars. One quarter now, and the remainder on delivery.'

'Alive?'

'I believe she has been taken by a raiding party of Mescalero Apaches. Therefore it will not be easy. That money if you bring positive proof of her death.'

'What if she's alive?'

The man shrugged. 'The same. It is of no consequence to me.'

Only then did Jed Herne ask the obvious question. 'Who is she?'

'My wife, Mister Herne. My name is Elisha Parsons.'

Chapter Three

It took the best part of a day for them to reach the Parsons spread. Ranging across a vast area of the New Mexico Territory, clean to the lower slopes of the Sierra Mogollon.

During that time, apart from offering the basic information that Jed needed, Parsons never spoke a word. Riding hard and tall in the saddle, on a hard-mouthed bay stallion, looking neither to right nor left.

He had brought a half dozen of his hands with him to Lordsburg, and they were as silent as their employer. Still, it made little difference to Herne. He was never a great one for conversation, and his first impression was that the man was still shocked by the loss of his pretty wife. And that was something with which Jed could sympathize. God knew he could.

But he quickly realized that there was more than that. Something he could only just begin to see, let alone understand. Jed had met a lot of angry and bitter men in his life, but never anyone quite as cold and self-contained as Elisha Parsons. He had to be a few years older than Herne, but he'd never come across him before. Heard the Parsons name, of course, as one of the biggest ranchers in the area, but never met him, or, as far as he could recall, even met anyone else who'd met him.

With that kind of self-control and an iron will, he guessed that Parsons could have become one of the great gunfighters, yet Herne had never even caught a bar-room whisper of the man using a gun. Maybe way back when he was winning his spread, but not for years. Parsons' way was to use the lawyers. Buy up a little here. Divert a river there, and then pick up the dried remnants of land for next to nothing. Day or so later that land had water again.

So it had gone, until the lots of little started to join up and look a lot. Once you got to be that big, it was all too easy to carry on getting even bigger.

And the woman looked, from the picture, a whole lot younger than Parsons. Jed Herne saw nothing wrong with that. His own sweet Louise, more than a year dead, had been only a child of sixteen when they met and married, and he had been just a few days past his thirty-fifth birthday. That marriage, for its short life, had been a good one for both of them.

Despite the near-silence of the hands that rode back with them from Lordsburg, it wasn't that difficult for Jed to get a vivid picture of the Parsons marriage. And it was an ugly picture.

Even before they reached the big house, Jed was ready for it. A great tomb of a house, with long passageways and huge rooms with high ceilings. Parsons a bitter man who had married youth wishing for sons, and had been given none. And a flighty wife who ran away at every chance, though the feeling seemed to be that old Lishe wouldn't let her get away with it again.

The hands went off to their own quarters, and Jed and his new employer entered the house. Despite the blazing heat of the day, it was as cold as charity inside. Jed looked around, expecting to see servants.

'We lost the right to keep slaves many years back, Herne. I will not have servants in my house while I am here, except for one man to wait on me. The rest work when I am out, which is much of the time.'

Jed went and sat down in one of the deep brocaded chairs by the empty fireplace, ignoring Parsons' glare at him for his temerity. 'I heard something about no more slaves too, Mister Parsons. And in passing, I'd like you to take a note that I am *Mister* Herne to you.'

'I see,' was all of the rancher's reply. He walked slowly over and sat across the Persian runner from Herne. Although Jed had guessed there wasn't that much in their ages, Parsons moved like a much older man. Stiff and steady, as if he feared a sudden movement might snap off an arm or a leg.

When he was comfortable, he looked at the gunman. And raised an eyebrow.

'What's up?'

'I was wondering, *Mister* Herne, if you were intending to try and find the woman by sitting there and hoping the Apaches would one day return her like a scythe or an axe that they have been borrowing.'

'Mister Parsons, I've seen nothin' yet that makes me like you. A lot that makes me not like you. But you've done a deal with me, and that's the way it'll be.'

'I've asked around, Mister Herne. They tell me that you are the best. That's what I need. I will not let that woman get away from me. I made her a promise, and I shall keep it.'

'Your wife went riding with your ramrod, four days back. Out in the foothills near Pinnacle Canyon. Never came back. And the local Fort have gotten word from scouts that a few Mescalero bucks have taken two prisoners. Whites. That's all you know?'

'That is all. My wife has tried to leave me before. I am not concerned with why the . . . why she left me. I will have her back. This time I will keep her. There will be no more freedom and rides for her. As long as she remains my wife, she will not leave the walls of this house ever again.'

It was the nearest to emotion that Herne had seen from the rancher.

'How you aim to keep her? Since we was both saying how you couldn't keep slaves no more?'

Parsons smiled. Another first in their relationship. Herne

couldn't recall when he'd seen such an unpleasant gloating smile. Parsons got up and walked to a heavy cupboard near the shuttered window. Unlocked it and flung the doors open for Herne to see. Even in the dim half-light, Jed could make out what was in there.

There had once been a wealthy whore in New Orleans called 'Whippin' Heather', and Jed had stayed with her a few times. Her speciality had been giving local shopkeepers and businessmen what she called 'correction'. Which meant a good flogging, while the clients were kept in chains. In her bedroom, Heather had a cupboard about the same size as the one in Parsons' parlour. With the same sort of contents. An assortment of snakeskin whips, and wrist shackles. Leg-irons. Neck collars of rusty iron. Manacles. Leg-spreaders. Spiked bars that fastened around the throat and made it impossible for the victim to lie down or feed himself.

Or herself.

'The time of slavery might have regrettably left us, Mister Herne, but our politicians do not yet presume to decide for us what a man may do with his wife in the privacy of his own home. I can promise you that Emmie-Lou will *never* run away from me again.'

There wasn't anything that Herne could do at the house. One of the women told him what the girl had been wearing. A pale blue shirt, over a black skirt. Riding boots. And, he supposed, some kind of under-pinnings. Probably made of horsehair, if her husband had any say in the matter.

Tanner, the ramrod, had disappeared with Emmie-Lou, and Herne wondered for a few minutes if the pair had skipped together. Until he heard how long Tanner and Parsons had known each other, and the total loyalty that the foreman had for his boss. It was still a remote possibility, but the Mescaleros seemed the best bet.

That meant going along to the local fort, and talking to

the officers there about the tribe that were on the move. Parsons had paid him his openers, and then simply left him to it. Apart from saying he expected either his wife or proof of her death within ten days.

Walking from the big house, Herne breathed deep of the hot afternoon air, glancing up at the sun. Looking back at the vault with its shuttered, blank windows. Checking that he still held the brown-tinted picture of the fresh young girl. Wrinkling his nose as he wondered if she was already dead. And if she wasn't, then what kind of a favour would he be doing her by returning her to her ... he almost thought 'owner'. To her husband?

The nearest fort would be Fort Gilman, forty miles from the longer established Fort McLane. The Commanding Officer was Major Corwin. That was where he'd go and that would be the man to ask. Then all he needed to do was find where the Mescaleros had taken Emmie-Lou Parsons, rescue her and deliver her back to her husband, collect the balance of the money and ride on. Another job.

He wished that he had Whitey Coburn with him, but the albino was dead. Buried beneath rock and snow high up in the Sierras.*

Whitey had always said being a top gun was like living in a huge house with hundreds of doors. So many doors that you can't believe that you'll ever reach the end. Every time you faced another man, you shut a door. Never seemed an end to those doors. Until one day you looked around the house, and they were all shut.

And that was the end.

(**See earlier books in the Herne series, also available from Corgi.*)

Chapter Four

Fort Gilman was like a dozen other forts in the South-West, holding together the fragile strands of white civilization through Arizona and New Mexico. Set way in the middle of nothing, with no hills or draws for hostiles to creep up under cover and burn them out. There were still soldiers serving in the Cavalry who remembered the stories of the great Apache warrior, Cuchillo Oro, of the golden knife, who had used cover to destroy a fort not two hundred miles from Fort Gilman.

The flag fluttered proudly in the late afternoon breeze, high over the parade-ground. The massive stockade of logs stood firm and four-square, though the days of Cuchillo Oro, himself the grandson of the mighty Mangas Colorado, and of hundreds of warriors in raiding parties were long gone. Now the worst that the settlers in the South-West had to fear was a sneak attack by a couple of dozen braves, out for glory or guns. Precisely the sort of attack that had taken Emmie-Lou Parsons and the ramrod, Tanner.

The news of the raiders had reached the Fort. Sentries had carried the word of an approaching rider minutes before Jed reached the closed gates, and the challenge was briskly delivered from over the barrel of a rifle. One white man might not be a threat, but it was a scant six years since George Custer had vanished along the snake-infested hills of the Little Big Horn River away to the north. And his command had died with him. No serving soldier would ever forget that.

'Halt. What's your name and business at Fort Gilman?'

'Name's Jedediah Herne, and I have business with your Major Corwin.'

A brief pause, and then the one gate swung open far enough for him to heel his mount forwards, closing immediately behind him. He whistled under his breath at the picture of neatness that met his eyes. The parade-ground was a perfect square of raked sand, surrounded by small white-painted blocks of stone.

Whoever Major Corwin was, he ran a tight fort. Herne was impressed. He'd visited a lot of Army camps, and never seen one that smelled so much of polish and discipline. A young officer came marching smartly out of one of the huts, and saluted him.

'I'm Lieutenant Cyrus Pinner, Sir. Can I be of any service to you?'

'Pinner?'

'Sir.'

'Ridin' in here I got to thinkin' about Apaches, and about old Golden Knife. My memory serves me right, but wasn't he also known as "Pinner's Indian"?'

The young officer flushed. 'My father, sir, was the officer who pursued a feud with the Mimbrenos Apache named Cuchillo Oro. Now if you'll follow me?'

It wasn't a subject to follow up, thought Herne, swinging down out of the saddle of his horse. The long-drawn out hatred between Cavalryman and Apache had been the talk of the frontier twenty or so years back, around the time of the great war.

It was cool in the office, and Herne blinked at the sudden darkness, seeing that Pinner had seated himself behind a desk. Looking up at him, waiting to know his business.

'Lieutenant. 'Fore I start, I'm sorry if I was tactless in mentioning your father and . . .'

There was a flash of a brief smile. 'I was always told that I should never apologize and that it was a . . .'

'Sign of weakness. Old Brittles may have joined his wife, but his words sure linger on after him.'

'I never knew my father, you see, what with him . . .'

'Sure. Let's forget it. The dead aren't interested in what we say about them, and I'm not that interested in the dead. Seen too many of them.'

'You're here because of the bucks taking the Parsons woman and the ramrod.'

'That's right. You're well informed.'

'The Major runs things in a tight way.'

'All ways?'

'What does that mean, Mister Herne?'

'Means that a nice raked parade-ground and splashes of white paint here and there don't mean that the men are what you need when your back's to the wall.'

Pinner didn't reply immediately. 'You saw the parade-ground? Guess you couldn't have failed to see it. That's Major Corwin's pride and joy. Some folks say he spends more time making sure it's clean and unspoilt than he does on finding out where the Mescalero men have gone and what they're doing. The previous Commanding Officer here was a good man. Kept a messy parade-ground, but the scouts were good and the patrols went out regular. Some of that still works, but some of it's gone.'

'You don't like it?'

'I like an Army that either fights or works hard at keeping the peace. Not just painting stones and putting them in damned little lines. I'm waiting for a transfer. Shouldn't run off at the mouth like this about my superior officer, but I've had it up to here, Mister Herne. Since the Apaches took the girl and the man, the scouts have told us where they are. And Corwin's done sweet damn-all about it. Says we wait and maybe they'll return her.'

'I see. So it's hardly likely I'll get a whole lot of help if I want to go in.'

The young officer shook his head. 'The Major will tell you how brave you are in attempting a rescue, and that he admires you and how much he wishes he had men like you under his command. In between asking if you saw his parade-ground, of course. He'll tell you that One Eye and his boys are . . .'

'One Eye?'

Pinner nodded. 'Right. Not the sort of Indian that you can introduce to a visiting Congressman.'

'Don't know much about him. Has he really only got one eye?'

'No. One eye brown like the rest of the tribe, and the other eye's blue. He and about forty braves are holed up in West Wind Canyon. It's on the far side of the foothills, and there's only one trail into it. You can get up to the head of it, but the cliffs down to where they're camped are sheer and close to a hundred feet high. And they guard that back trail too well for a surprise.'

'Box canyon. Sort of place where a couple of men with repeaters could hold off the whole of the Cavalry.'

'Right. I figure you'll get an escort there. And maybe one back if you make it. But the Major won't risk a frontal attack in case he loses too many men. One Eye doesn't do that much harm.'

'Taking a white girl, and killing white men! What the Hell kind of trouble does the Major want!'

The door swung open, and an irritable voice answered him. 'My officers being disloyal behind my back? Not what I want, Mister Pinner. Shame you're not the man your father was. I'm Corwin, and you're Herne the Hunter. The bounty-seeking gunman.'

Herne faced the senior officer, seeing the sort of man that he'd expected from Lieutenant Pinner's description.

Short, barely touching five feet four inches tall. Narrow in the shoulder and broad in the hip. With a spreading gut that told of too much of the soft life. An immaculate uniform that must have come from a very expensive military tailor, with highly-polished brass and silver. The collar supported two or three chins more than the average man, and the cheeks glowed with the kind of rude good health that only comes out of the bottom of shot glasses.

The eyes were close together, half-buried in layers of soft pink fat, like black marbles. At his unexpected entrance, Lieutenant Pinner sprang to his feet, cracking off a salute that snapped the air with its violence. He made no attempt to reply to the charge of disloyalty, clearly knowing from experience that Major Corwin was not a man to listen to argument.

'I would say that the Lieutenant was being most helpful. Far from speaking in a disloyal manner, Major Corwin, he was telling me of your exploits in a manner that would have set your ears burning had you overheard them.'

'Was he?'

'Indeed, and he was paying special attention to that magnificent stretch of smooth ground over there, alongside the flagpole. It must take you hours of personal attention.'

Corwin was so subject to flattery that he failed to recognize the sarcasm. 'My parade-ground is the one great pride of my life. All my military career, Mister Herne, it has been my ambition to have a parade-ground that would be perfection. No more and no less. Finally, I have it here at Fort Gilman, after nearly two years of hard work for all of us,' Herne saw Pinner unable to check the elevation of an eyebrow. 'But we have made the square here the finest in the South-West. I would go further. The finest in the whole damn country. And we all know that means just about the best in the world. If anything tarnished or spoilt its surface, I believe it would destroy me.'

'How do the men get to the flagpole to raise and lower the flag?'

'They cross wearing special soft shoes, and return with a party of men whose sole function at the Fort is to dust and smooth that ground. Pretty damned impressive. Bet you've never seen anything like that before?'

Herne shook his head solemnly. 'Hand on heart, Major Corwin, and I can swear I have never even *heard* of anything like that before.'

The private meeting with Major Alexander Corwin was more or less as young Lieutenant Pinner had predicted. Filled to overflowing with self-importance and caution, he was very sorry to hear about the kidnapping of the wife of such an important man as Elisha Parsons, but what could he do?

'Ride in and bring her and the ramrod back out,' was Herne's suggestion.

'Not enough men trained in fighting hostile Indians,' was Corwin's reply.

'What about any trained in fighting with friendly ones?' said Herne, beginning to lose his patience.

'Good one that, Mister Herne. Must remember it. No, the Mescaleros trapped in West Wind Canyon can do little harm and in due time they will surrender to us and the girl will probably be spared.'

'Damn it, Major!' Jed's anger finally boiled to the surface. 'Have you no idea at all what Apaches can do to a white woman? By now the man Tanner will almost certainly be dead. Tortured by the women of the tribe. And Mrs. Parsons is not likely to have had an easy time at their hands.'

'I'm sorry,' shrugged Corwin, his face giving the lie to his words. 'I've been trying to get them out of that box canyon for months, but I'm not prepared to lose another patrol trying to charge in with flags flying and bugles blowing.'

The word 'another' registered on Herne, but he made no comment. Pinner was standing quietly at the back of the office, and the two men's eyes met. It was easy to understand why the young Lieutenant was so anxious to get a transfer away from the spick and span Fort Gilman.

'But you can help me, Mister Herne. Indeed you can. I'll hold the front and stage a diversion. Give you time to sneak in round the back. Then you can do the same for me. I'll feint a withdrawal. You fire a few wigwams and they'll come back inside leaving the entrance without a guard.'

'Wickiups, sir.'

'What was that, Lieutenant?'

'Wickiups, sir. The Apache tribes do not live in wigwams. They live in wickiups. Earth and . . .'

Corwin flushed, banging his chubby fist pettishly on his desk. 'I know what a wickiup is. And that was what I said. You, Lieutenant Pinner, may go and superintend the evening patrol of the parade-ground. This wind that's getting up will mean a double raking for it tonight.'

Saluting, his face a mask of self-control, Pinner marched from the room. Corwin enlarged on his plan, obviously seeing Herne as manna from heaven in giving him an easy entry to the canyon and a simple victory over One Eye and the rest of his band.

Jed didn't see it that way. Apart from having to stalk his way into a guarded camp, and bring out the girl and possibly the man, he wasn't minded to waste time on starting fires. But it was better not to tell Corwin that. A diversion at the mouth of West Wind Canyon might be of some use in helping him to get in, but the Mescaleros were hardly likely to rush about with panic and leave their front door gaping open just because of a little smoke. It was a ridiculous plan.

'You like the idea, Mister Herne?'

He grinned and stood up. 'Like it about as much as I do your parade-ground and your Fort, Major. And that's really saying something.'

Corwin beamed at him. 'Then we'll do it.'

'Right. Tomorrow, we'll do it. First light.'

'Well.'

'What's wrong?'

'Always like to check before doing anything else in the morning that all's well with . . .'

'The parade-ground!'

'Right, Mister Herne. Habit of a lifetime is a hard one to break.'

'For Mrs. Parsons, the only habit that she's going to find important is the one of living.'

'I guess I could make an exception.'

Herne stood closer to the small man, leaning over him so that his shadow blotted out most of the light from the gleaming window.

'Guess you could, at that, Major. Be right neighbourly of you.'

'We'll have "Boots and Saddles" at two. Means we'll get there just before sun-up.'

'That's fine. I'll snatch some sleep. Hope to be on the back trail to West Wind Canyon by around four tomorrow.'

He was within sight of the sentries by eight minutes after four.

Chapter Five

It was still dark.

The Cavalry patrol that Corwin had sent out had ridden with all the inconspicuous skill of a rattlesnake in a bowl of cranberry sauce. Herne would have been the first to recognize the problems of a largish body of men on horseback travelling quietly and without being seen by Mescalero scouts. But he didn't feel it was necessary for the patrol to have left the Fort with the whole regimental trimmings. Turning out the band at a little after midnight, playing 'Garryowen' so that everyone for miles would know the Cavalry were moving out.

There were twenty-eight troopers, with an experienced sergeant, and young Lieutenant Pinner in command. Major Corwin had finally decided that he wouldn't lead the patrol himself, having more pressing business back at the Fort. Jed had no doubt that the business would be concerned with repainting the window-frame the right shade of brown, or ensuring that every man still had the regulation knife, fork and spoon. Important things like that. Or maybe checking nobody had accidentally trodden on the hallowed square of the parade-ground.

Herne had left his horse the best part of a mile back, having the disadvantage of not being able to check out the lay of the ground for himself, though Pinner had been a lot of help, making a rough map and a sketch plan for him of the way into West Wind Canyon.

It led a long way around the rear of the box canyon, through an area known as the Devil's Playground. It was a common name in Arizona and New Mexico for that type of terrain. A great jumbled mass of fiery boulders, scattered wilfully about in tortuous shapes and random patterns. With a narrow trail winding in among them, rising gradually towards the looming top of the arroyo.

From there on in, Pinner was more hazy. 'Nobody ever got in that way and out again, far as I know. It's a tough climb to the top, and you'll have to get by the Mescalero guards. Then it's an even steeper climb down into the camp. We'll be here,' pointing to the clear area around the opening to the steep-sided draw. 'I'll ring it, and when we see the smoke from the fire, we'll all come a'running. Try and give you cover to get out with whoever's still alive.'

'And cover to take them away after first light?'

'Right. Mister Herne?' There was a questioning note of doubt in the young man's voice.

'What is it?'

'This plan. You don't think maybe that the Major's aiming to . . . kind of . . .'

'Wheel and deal on me? Use me to do what he's never had the guts to do himself?'

'I wouldn't want it thought, Mister Herne, that those were the sentiments of a junior serving officer in the Cavalry of the United States of America, concerning my superior. That would be disloyalty.'

'But you can think it, just the same. I know it and so do you.'

Pinner frowned. 'I'd just say that I wouldn't count too much on everything being like the Major says it is.'

Herne had grinned.

'Major thinks he's using me as a way of getting rid of One Eye and his band. Doesn't occur to him maybe I'm just using him as a way of getting in there. What I do when I'm in there'll depend on what I find. If'n I get time, and I doubt I will, then you'll see a whole lot of smoke.'

And so they'd left it. First light would be around five, and by then Herne wanted to be close enough to knock over the sentry. Or sentries. Trail like that could easily be watched by one man, but if One Eye was any use as a leader, then he'd have taken the precaution of doubling up.

Fifteen minutes after five and Pinner and his men would ride around the opening to the Canyon, yelling and shooting and making enough noise to convince the Apaches that it was a genuine attack on their stronghold. That should distract them from checking out their guards on the rear entrance to the camp.

That was the theory.

Now, huddled against the morning chill behind a massive boulder, was the time to put it into practice. The time to think through your next move, and check your weapons.

The honed bayonet – a relic from Jed's days with Quantrill's raiders – stuck down the inside of the right boot, in its own sheath. The Sharps rifle stayed in its bucket with the horse, back out of sight. It was a great gun if you wanted to pick a man off a wall at a quarter mile, but not a lot of use in the mission that Herne was on. If there was going to be any shooting, and there probably was, then the well-worn Colt would be what was needed. Something to stop a man at twenty yards.

He squinted up the hill, along where the faint ghost of the trail wound out of sight. There was the pale sliver of a young moon, sinking out of sight. And the first touch of light, signalling the false dawn that was coming closer. Time to stop the thinking and get on with the moving.

The Devil's Playground was a tortured landscape, with its rocks baked by the New Mexico sun and frozen by the cold of the nights. During the day they would be too hot to touch, and now they were as cold as a drowned corpse. Jed slithered his way among them, gun in its holster, and knife in its sheath. He was backing himself to beat even a Mescalero by hearing them before they heard him.

Noise would carry a mile or more in the stillness and to try and sneak up on armed guards with either the Colt or the bayonet in his hand would have vastly increased the risk of an accidental sound.

In the past, Jed had fought against many of the more troublesome Indian tribes. Sioux and Cheyenne. Arapaho and Apache. But he'd never been involved in a mission on his own, trying to get in and out of a closely-guarded camp.

'It's only money,' he whispered to himself, thinking in the

solitary darkness of the solemn-faced girl eight thousand miles away in an English school. Rebecca Yates, her gentle and orthodox British education depending on his own skill with the bullet and blade. Her French and Latin paid for by the blood of other men. Maybe, ultimately, by his own blood.

Step by silent step, feeling his way forwards as the path steepened, keeping low against the boulders, ears straining for the first clue. The sound that would tell him where the enemy were.

If he had been responsible for that back trail to the Canyon, he would have put three guards to it. Two at the top, and his best man half-way down. He was nearly at the top, able to see the glow of cooking fires from the other side of the ridge, before he saw the sentries.

Two of them, close together. Sitting by a small fire, huddled under blankets, the barrels of their rifles sticking up against the red light of the flames. Heads leaning forwards, deep in conversation. As Herne crawled closer still, he caught the low sound of their talking.

He had to take a gamble, on whether there might be a change of the the sentries before dawn. But it was more likely that they would change around the time the camp came to life and the first food of the day was served. So that the new men could eat and then make the steep climb up to the look-out point to relieve the guards from the night.

It was a gamble, as he would be dead if he met the replacement warriors on their way up, while he was on the way down. But it was a gamble that he had to take. There wasn't any choice.

For several long minutes, Jed Herne remained quite still, eyes never leaving the two men. Trying in that short time to get into the minds of two young Mescalero warriors. Guessing what kind of men they were. How alert they would be to any movement around them.

Suddenly, the one to his right stood up, and walked straight towards the boulder where he was crouching. Herne's bayonet whispered from its sheath, gleaming dully in the reflected light of the dying fire. The Apache was still wrapped in the blanket, his rifle trailing in the right hand. Jed knew that he couldn't have been seen, so . . .?

The answer came soon enough. When he was a few paces from the hiding white man, the Indian stopped. He bent down and laid his rifle silently on the path, then straightened and turned away from his comrade by the fire. And loosened his belt, letting down white cotton trousers. Laying the blanket alongside him as he squatted behind a large rock.

It was a lucky break, and Jed hadn't lived as long as he had by missing up on such chances. He ghosted from his hiding-place, one eye on the other sentry who remained crouched by the fire. The bayonet probing at the darkness in front of him, Herne moved forwards.

The Mescalero had just finished what he had been doing, and was standing up, the pale moons of his buttocks clearly visible. Herne made his move, taped hilt of the knife gripped in his right hand. Powering his way across the few steps of sand that separated them. Left arm snaking around the shorter man's neck, clamping across the wind-pipe like a band of steel. Tightening and lifting, bringing the Mescalero clear off the ground, his jaw open, breath croaking in his throat as he fought silently for his life.

Turning his left hip slightly, to brace the struggling man against him, Herne the Hunter brought his right arm across his stomach. Felt delicately with the point of the knife for the correct place. The Mescalero jerked as the needle-tip pierced his skin. With a quick half-step, Jed turned his opponent so that the whole of his back was a target for the bayonet.

The pale colour of the Indian's cotton shirt helped. The blade hissed in, thrust with all of Jed's strength, angling up between the left ribs, and slicing through the walls of the Apache's heart, killing him almost instantly. The body jerked and kicked, but Jed held on, keeping his arm locked round the man's neck, squeezing tightly to prevent any sound which would warn the second sentry.

Only when the corpse hung still and limp did he relax his grip, pulling out the knife and letting the body slide gently to the earth. He wiped the warm blood from the blade, and stood up again, eyes searching for the other guard.

He was still sitting huddled over the fire, clutching his rifle. He half-turned as the body shifted, disturbing the layer of tiny pebbles on the trail, and called out. Something that Herne hoped didn't require an answer, as he was too far from the man to hope to take him silently, and a shot would bring a dozen armed warriors scrambling up after him. He'd get away without any great problem, but it would mean the end of any chance of rescue for Emmie-Lou Parsons. And that meant the end of his own chance of picking up the balance of the bounty from her loving husband.

Eighteen hundred and seventy-five dollars would buy a term's schooling with enough left over for him to live a few weeks, and maybe think about buying a new mount.

But all that was in the future. Whitey Coburn used to say that a gunman who started worrying about his future would wake up one morning to find that he hadn't got one.

It was very quiet on top of the spur, with only the faintest breath of wind stirring the night air. Far away to the east, the false dawn had vanished, but it was being replaced by the pink glow of the sun-rise. Another few minutes and it would begin to lighten.

Just as he started forward, knife flicking out in front of him like a snake's tongue, the scream tore at the blackness. So despairing and lonesome that it racked at the ears, and made the night that much colder. It was a blind and insensate cry, seeking help where there could not possibly be any.

High and thin, wailing away into the desert, and bouncing from crag to crag of the Mogollons. Pain of a shuddering desolate kind was in the scream, and Herne closed his eyes for a moment, trying to shut out the noise as it rasped on and on. Rising and falling, and finally sliding down the scale to a low, almost liquid bubbling.

He'd heard that sort of noise before, and knew what it was. Unless they'd caught any other whites, it meant that the ramrod, Tanner, was nearing the end of the line.

The guard also heard the noise – so loud that it must even have carried to the waiting troopers – and he stood up and walked nearer to the edge of the drop to the camp, shouting something back to his comrade.

Laughing at the suffering scream.

Wild anger blazed in Herne's mind at the callous and brutal indifference to the pain of others, and he came as close as he had come for many years to reverting to the blind fury of his youth. He was filled with a burning desire to leap on the unsuspecting Mescalero and beat him to the stones. Pound and crush that face and laughing mouth to a bloody pulp, and then throw the corpse over the cliff.

But the calmness of reason inched back, and he stood still, shaking slightly with the effort, hands down at his sides while he took a half dozen deep breaths. Only when he knew he was again under control did he stare through the dimness, seeing the man still shrouded in his blanket, looking down over West Wind Canyon.

It was a dozen steps to the guard, and he took them at close to a normal pace, putting his trust in the fact that the man might turn at any moment, but would probably think the grating of boots on the sandy stones came from his returning brother. It was a reasonable thing to think, with the food waiting for him down in the village, and sleep not far off.

He began his turn as Herne reached his shoulder, but

never completed it. The left hand pulled at the Apache's hair, jerking him off balance, while the razor-edge of the old bayonet hacked through his throat, drowning the cry for help in a welter of blood.

The man struggled so hard against the red flood of death that a great clump of his lank hair was ripped from his skull, and it took all of Herne's strength to stop the Mescalero from toppling over the edge of the ravine and alerting the whole camp to his presence.

Finally the fountain became a trickle, and the arms and legs hung limply. Jed lowered the blood-sodden corpse to the stones, wiping the bayonet on one of the few remaining clean patches of the Apache's shirt. Rubbed his hands dry of the grease from the hair, and stood up, taking several deep breaths to ready himself for the next stage of the attempted rescue.

After that one scream, there had been more or less total silence from the camp. Peering down into the black cauldron of West Wind Canyon, he could see the red dots of the fires, and the dark outlines of the couple of dozen wickiups, scattered around the bottom of the boxed end. Away behind him the sky was still lightening, as the dawn grew closer.

Although everything was still going according to plan, Herne knew that time was slipping inexorably away from him. The narrow path down the rocky walls of the Canyon would be difficult enough to climb in the darkness, but it would be fatal to try and claw his way down in the light. He took out his silver half-hunter and peered at it, turning it so that the fingers reflected the faint light of morning.

It was close to five. In a little over a quarter of an hour, Pinner would be starting his diversion, and the Apache camp would be humming like a hive of angry bees. When that happened, Herne wanted to be close to the camp, ready to move in.

He stepped cautiously closer to the brink of the drop,

seeing the path winding down below him for a few feet, before it disappeared into the darkness. It would not be an easy climb in daylight. At night it would be damnably dangerous.

Making sure that the thong across the hammer held his Colt safely in the holster, he began the descent, picking his way with silent care among the boulders and crags of the sandstone mountain.

The information from the Cavalry had been pretty accurate. It was around a hundred feet straight down, and that would be more than enough to spread him very thin. Herne had never been fond of heights, and he felt a momentary dizziness as he paused about twenty feet from the top. The trail snaked backwards and forwards across the face of the cliff, picking its way among the jutting knives of stone.

The light was improving fast, and he could now see a couple of figures moving in the gloom of the camp. Squaws, getting ready for the first meal. Probably tepary beans, with a little butter. Or a chili stew with blue corn bread. He imagined that he could smell it, rising from the depths below him, and he grinned ruefully to himself, wishing he'd brought some jerky with him to stave off the pangs of hunger.

He was just rounding one of the great hanging outcrops that nearly blocked the pathway, his mind drifting away to thoughts of food.

When he bumped straight into the Apache warrior carrying a rifle.

Chapter Six

Part of Herne's mind was thinking about the food. Which lost him a little of the edge he should have had. But there was a difference in the two men's reaction times to the confrontation. The Apache was still sleepy, clambering stolidly up the pathway to relieve the two night sentries. For in the day it would be impossible for anyone to get within two miles of the Canyon without being spotted from the top.

In all the time that the Mescalero Indians had camped in West Wind Canyon nobody had ever attempted to scale the heights and attack from the rear. So he was quite unprepared for a meeting with a white man on the pathway. Although Herne cursed himself for letting his concentration slip, he was at least partly prepared for a chance encounter with one of the Apaches. Which made his response that vital fraction of a second quicker than the warrior.

The light was racing across the land, and Herne could clearly see the man's face as he started to react to the presence of the intruder on the path. His jaw began to open, and the rifle was on the way up from low down. Too low down to have a chance against a man of the calibre of Herne the Hunter.

Both men had taken an instinctive step backwards at the encounter, Jed going for the Colt – and finding the hammer snagged by the leather thong that held it safe while he was climbing. Fumbling with it cost a valuable half second, giving the Indian time to bring the Winchester up, right hand going for the trigger, right thumb groping for the hammer.

Even as he finally got his own pistol clear of the leather,

Jed knew that he'd lost the war, even though he reckoned he'd win the battle. By shooting the Mescalero, he would wake up the entire camp, and that would end his chances of getting in to rescue Emmie-Lou Parsons. That lone despairing scream had told him that Tanner would be beyond any help of any man.

The speed of the white man's draw froze the stretched smile of triumph on the face of the squat Apache. He had never thought it would have been possible for Herne to reach for his Colt and level it before the Winchester blasted him from the path to the hunting-ground of the white-eyes. Yet the hammer of the rifle had barely begun to move back and already he was staring down the gaping barrel of the hand-gun.

'Sorry,' said Herne, squeezing the narrow trigger of the Colt, feeling its familiar kick against the wrist. But his regret wasn't for the Apache, who would have shot him if he had taken his chance, but for the pretty young girl who must now be left behind him.

The bullet hit the warrior in the centre of the chest, splintering its way through his breast-bone, angling off into his lungs and exiting beneath the right shoulder. The force of the blow sent him staggering backwards, cannoning off the red-tinted boulder, leaving a brighter splash of red across it. The rifle clattered from his hands, sliding a few feet and then stopping on the edge of the drop.

His fingers clamped on the entrance hole of the bullet, trying to force the life back within his body, half-leaning and half-falling, bracing himself with his unwounded shoulder, eyes flat and expressionless, lips opening and closing like those of an old man.

At such close range, Herne had been forced by safety to go for a body shot, though it would always take longer to kill a man than a bullet in the head. Now the Apache might take a minute or longer to die. Jed glanced down, peeping cautiously over the top of the rocks, seeing the effect that the shot had caused in the Mescalero village. As he had expected it brought men and woman pouring from their wickiups, shouting and gesticulating.

He suddenly realized that they couldn't tell where the shot had come from, masked behind the rocks, so high above them, echoing and swirling around the Canyon, making it quite impossible to locate.

The dying man made a great effort to reach his knife, letting the blood flow unchecked from his chest, soaking through the flowered cotton shirt. He blinked several times, as though he was trying to clear a mist from his eyes, and took a faltering step from the support of the boulder. Herne knew that a second shot would give his position away, and held back, hoping that he might at least have a free climb back to safety.

Then two things happened simultaneously which altered his plans in a dramatic fashion.

The damage to the torn tissue of his lungs was suddenly too much for the Apache, who dropped to his knees, bright red blood frothing from his mouth and spurting down his nose, across his chin, and pattering into the dry sand. His hands reached out, like a penitent agonizing for a touch of a religious relic, then slipped gently forward, like a swimmer entering deep water, lying very still with the tips of his fingers only inches from Herne's feet.

And at the same moment, Jed heard a crackle of shots, spitting and bouncing around the Canyon. He ducked down, imagining that he'd been seen, realizing immediately that it wasn't that. There was none of the noise of bullets striking and screeching away off rocks anywhere near him.

So that meant . . .

'Quarter after five. Right on the nail, Lieutenant. Better'n you can guess,' he said to nobody in particular.

Now that the feint had begun, the Apaches would be running to defend their front door, and would think that the shot Herne had just fired had come from the Cavalry patrol. There wouldn't be any reason for them to suspect their escape route had been infiltrated.

Carefully, keeping as flat and as low as possible, he began to creep down the path, watching as the Apaches scattered out across the wide head of the Canyon, making their way towards the narrow neck, where they would be occupied for a while holding off the Cavalry. The camp was quietening, with the women going on with their business. Carrying washing to the small stream that flowed from the bottom of the cliff where he climbed. A clump of trees surrounded the pool, close to the nearest of the wickiups.

Four or five squaws, stout and shapeless in their long fringed dresses, driving another woman in front of them. Even from his high-up position, Herne couldn't have failed to recognize the naked figure of the white woman. It was Emmie-Lou Parsons, carrying a pile of clothes towards the pool, goaded on by the Indian women, who each had a sharp stick with which they prodded her. Her pale skin was blotched with dirt, and bruised across the breasts and hips, with spots of blood here and there from the points of the sticks.

Twice while he watched, still making his careful and secretive way nearer, Herne saw the white woman stumble and nearly fall. The squaws laughed and jeered her, quite oblivious to the gun-battle that raged a quarter-mile away down the Canyon. They seemed to know that their retreat was invulnerable, and they ignored the shooting.

There was a charred tree close by the pool, with a bundle of burned sticks lashed to it. A small fire still glowed at the base of the tree, a curl of smoke twisting silently up from the embers. As they passed the bundle of sticks, each of the squaws poked at it with their makeshift spears. One of them stopping and lashing at the charred bundle with all of her strength, calling out to the others.

Herne felt the skin crawl on his back. The black sticks had moved! Cried out in a voice that was so feeble and thin it hardly seemed human.

Not only had Herne found the missing Emmie-Lou Parsons. He'd also just found what remained of the ramrod, Tanner.

If One Eye was any good as a leader, it wouldn't take him all that long to realize that the attacking force didn't really have it in mind to do any actual attacking. Then he'd start wondering about what sort of a diversion it was. And why.

So Herne had to keep on moving. He got a bonus when three of the five squaws left to go back to their own wickiups, leaving Emmie-Lou guarded by the remaining couple, one of whom, Jed noticed as he crept closer, was carrying a Winchester under her arm.

The trees gave him good cover, and the rushing stream shrouded any noise he might have made as he stalked towards his prey. There was a gap of fifteen or twenty yards between the nearest rock and the first of the trees. He waited as long as he dared for the camp to become empty. But there were always several squaws, and a dozen brats playing in the dust.

If he ran he would draw attention to himself, so he simply pulled out his shirt, and walked slowly across, keeping his face turned away, hoping that a casual glance would mistake him for one of the Apaches. He was nearly in the trees when he heard, and saw out of the corner of one eye, an Apache child point in his direction and call something out.

Like a ball from a musket, he leaped the last two or three steps, standing panting in the cooler shade of the glade, peering out through the green curtain of leaves, Colt ready drawn. The little naked boy who had seen him was pointing and the women were staring where he showed them. Jed stood very still, not even thumbing back the hammer on the gun in case its triple click should give him away.

One of the squaws, who Herne guessed was the mother of the little boy, obviously decided that her son was trying to trick them and wagged an angry finger at him. The rest of the women laughed and the little boy scampered away from them. Herne watched him, in case he tried to prove he'd really seen what he claimed, but the child seemed to have forgotten all about it and wandered off alone among the wickiups on the far side of the camp.

Among the trees he could hear the two women talking and sniggering. He walked like a ghost between the trunks, setting his foot down as carefully as if he was walking across eggs, looking straight ahead.

'Please. Please leave me alone! I'm trying! Oh, Blessed Jesus, I'm trying!!' Followed by tears, and renewed laughter from the Indian women.

There they were. Emmie-Lou, naked and very beautiful, kneeling down and trying to wash a cotton shirt between two large stones on the edge of a clear pool, made by damming the stream. The Mescalero women, one of whom was barely a teenager, stood and watched her. The white woman's long hair dangled across her shoulder, and she paused to push it up out of her eyes. The younger squaw screeched out at her, and reinforced her words with two cracking blows across the back, raising red weals on the tender skin.

The other Apache woman – the one with the rifle – stepped forward and took the shirt from Emmie-Lou's fingers. She looked at it contemptuously, then dropped it on the earth at the pool's edge and trampled on it until it was filthy and muddy, then handed it back to her accompanied by a slap across the face.

'Time to move in on the laundry,' said Herne quietly to

himself, taking the step beyond the trees that put him into clear view of the pool.

Both Indian women had their backs to him, but Emmie-Lou glanced up, attracted by the movement. The face was much like the face in the picture, but it seemed to have aged and grown hard. There was a livid bruise under the left eye, and a brown thread of dried blood at the corner of the mouth.

Holding the gun steady, Herne raised his left hand to his lips in a gesture of warning. He hoped that he could get closer to the other women and maybe take them out without noise.

It was a futile hope.

'Oh, thank God!' exclaimed Mrs. Parsons, half-standing, eyes wide open as if she couldn't believe what she saw.

An expression that was mirrored on the faces of the two Mescalero squaws as they spun round to see the tall figure of the white man, like some avenging spirit sprung from the soul of the trees, gun in hand and cold death in his eyes.

'Come to me, Mrs. Parsons. Slow and easy.'

Seeing the angel of salvation, Emmie-Lou suddenly became conscious that she was stark naked, and one hand flew to cover her breasts, while the other dropped to cover the dark triangle of matted hair at the junction of her thighs.

'No time for modesty, Mrs. Parsons. Just keep on walking towards . . . Bitch!!'

The older of the two women, carrying the rifle, suddenly screamed at the top of her voice, and came running at him, holding the Winchester like a lance. He saw her finger whiten on the trigger and shot her through the centre of the forehead, the bullet lifting her off her feet, throwing her backwards in a tangle of arms and legs. The rifle went up in the air in a lazy arc, lodging in the branches of one of the shady trees.

The second squaw also started towards him, changing her mind as she saw what happened to her companion. She hurled her stick at Herne, missing by only a hand's span, then dived into the water, vanishing in a cloud of white spray.

Herne steadied himself, holding his right wrist with his left hand for extra support, and waited until the girl's head and shoulders rose above the surface. As it did so he put a bullet carefully through the back of the skull, taking away most of her face as it exited. The body jerked and kicked for a few seconds, then floated serenely on the clear water, blood clouding out from the fatal wound.

'Get the dress off that first one,' snapped Herne to Emmie-Lou. 'And get a damned move on before the whole damned tribe gets on our asses.'

For a moment he thought that his prize was going to give out on him with a fit of the vapours. He took a half-step towards her, but she shook her head, and turned her back to him, bending down over the corpse of the Mescalero squaw, quickly ripping the dress off her.

'Just put it on anyhow. Don't stop to take mind of how it looks!'

Behind, from the direction of the camp, he could hear the voices of women, growing nearer. Excited and shouting. Even against the background of the shooting at the mouth of West Wind Canyon, the scream had been heard. His best hope was that none of the braves were there.

While Emmie-Lou dressed, tugging the damp skins over her nakedness, Herne quickly reloaded the Colt. Three bullets. Three kills. Economical shooting.

'I'm ready. Where do . . .?'

'No questions. Just stick closer to me than paint to a door and we'll make it.'

'What about Pete?'

'Who the . . .?'

'Pete Tanner. They've been doing . . . dreadful . . .'

'Yeah. I heard a mite of that while I was coming down the path this morning, 'fore sun-up. What they've done to Pete Tanner is done. Can't do nothing for him.'

'Look out!!'

Herne spun and fired in the same action, catching the movement from the edge of his vision. Someone with a drawn bow. One of the Mescaleros. The bullet made it four in a row. It smashed the bow in half, and carried on to tear clean through the chest of the Apache holding it, knocking him into one of the trees, and leaving him a bleeding corpse.

'Hell!' said Herne, angry at his own speed.

He had just shot the little boy who had pointed him out earlier. A little boy who would have been all of six.

He tried to back away from the oncoming women, keeping Emmie-Lou at his side, waving the gun at them in the vain hope that he wouldn't have to slaughter any more of the squaws or their brats.

'Shoot them down!' hissed Emmie-Lou at his elbow. 'Make them pay for what they did to me and Pete.'

'Guess they done a little of that already, Mrs. Parsons,' he replied.

But the women took the matters to themselves, coming after him with sticks. Butchering a mob of Apache women wasn't Jed's idea of gunfighting, but he knew well enough that a woman with a knife could kill a man as efficiently as a marksman with a Sharps rifle. He'd seen the bitch-queen of Memphis, Fat Alice Birch, prove that when she cut the throat of Linus May all over the floor of the Golden Flower saloon. Linus had always been squeamish about women, and couldn't bring himself to pull the trigger of his big forty-four.

Finest hanging Memphis had in years, with Fat Alice

blowing kisses to the crowd all the way to the gallows, and only the hangman spoiling things by figuring that Alice was a mite lighter than she really was. Might have been trying to be a gentleman, but all it did was pull her blonde head clean off her shoulders when the trap opened. Front eight rows got soaked in the blood.

If the squaws had been white women, Jed would have taken a chance on trying to talk them out of it. But they weren't, and he wouldn't.

'Get back!!' he shouted, waving the Colt at them, while Mrs. Parsons cowered behind him, still muttering for him to kill them all for what they'd done to her and Tanner.

He took no notice of her, and the women took no notice of him, surging forwards in a screaming bunch, with a few of the children scurrying around their skirts, throwing stones at him.

'God Damn,' Herne said quietly, firing four quick shots at the leading four women, aiming to stop them rather than slaughter them. Two went down holding smashed knees, and one clutching her stomach. The fourth snap shot missed the front rank, taking out one of the squaws at the rear, opening up a wide flesh wound under her ribs.

It stopped them. They all stood in a huddle, around the fallen women, their screaming and cursing muted, within twenty paces of Herne. He stood at the edge of the bloodied pool, watching them carefully, and slowly reloaded his Colt.

'Trail out goes up the path behind us. Through the trees and round the side of the nearest wickiup. Go on. Get a start and I'll join you. Shout if you see any bucks coming back to find out what all the shootin' is round here. Move it!'

Emmie-Lou Parsons started away from him, but he was aware that she was walking slowly. Jed risked a glance back, seeing her still on his side of the water, watching the action with frightened eyes.

'Get your ass out of here, or we're both dead. And keep low on the path!' he bellowed at her.

Another stone splashed in the water behind him, and Jed reckoned that it was also time for him to be moving. It wouldn't be long before some of the squaws remembered that there were guns in the wickiups, and came after him and the escaping captive.

Two more shots broke them. This time he fired to kill, picking them off like shooting fish in a barrel, knocking them over in the sand, which was being trampled up and soaked in blood until it resembled crimson mud. Leaving the two corpses behind, and the one gut-shot rolling about and screaming, the others fled, helping away the three injured women who could be moved.

Herne followed them up, firing a couple more shots over their heads to keep them on the move. Sending them scurrying and moaning away across the open space by the cooking fires, into the wickiups. Dragging their children behind them, feet trailing in the dust. In seconds, Herne stood alone in the middle of the Mescalero camp.

Not quite alone.

He was at the edge of the clump of trees, nearly within touching distance of the burned tree where the remains of Tanner hung, the small fire at his feet still smouldering gently. The air was heavy at that spot with the sickly-sweet scent of burning flesh.

The thing tied there made a noise. A low, regular sound. Herne doubted if there was anything left that could be called life, and that Tanner was no longer aware of anything going on around him. Not even aware that he was making a slow, hissing, rasping noise with every other breath. His world would have been filled with pain. Topped up and up until it overflowed and there was nothing but pain. That was when the brain would have given up.

There was hardly an inch of the naked body that wasn't

scorched black, the skin hanging in swollen blisters and tatters. Against the darkness, Herne could see speckles of fresh blood, shockingly clean and red, coming from where the squaws had beaten him as they passed by with Mrs. Parsons.

Suddenly Herne was glad that he'd killed the women. His only regret that he hadn't shot them all down. Wiped them out with the same disregard that they'd shown their helpless white prisoner.

For a moment he even thought of going on into their wickiups and gunning them all down. But time was running out. He had noticed that the crackle of firing from the neck of West Wind Canyon was slackening. That meant the Apaches were realizing that the attack wasn't going to be pressed home. Soon some of them would be back to check that all was well in their camp.

Major Corwin had told him to burn them out. *Told* him. Not even asked. And Herne the Hunter had never been the sort of man to do what he was told. Nobody ever threw him his guns and ordered him to run. So there would be no fire. He'd been hired to bring out the woman, and that was what he'd do. In any case, the earth huts of the Apaches wouldn't burn that easily, as Corwin ought to have known.

Tanner shifted in his bonds, and cried out. An unintelligible jumble of garbled sounds. Elisha Parsons had said that the ramrod had known about the threat from the Mescalero raiding party before he set out with Emmie-Lou, but that he'd been ready to take the chance.

Now he was near death. Herne knew enough of the ways of Apache squaws to guess without looking too closely what horrors lay beneath the roasted exterior. The tongue and the ear-drums would have gone early. And the ears themselves, and the eye lids. The lips, and all of the teeth. The nose sliced away. The genitals removed. If he had been lucky, they would have been cut quickly away with one slash of a skinning knife. Probably though, Tanner hadn't been lucky.

Finger-nails, and then the fingers themselves. Each one bent slowly back, until it cracked while the women would all have laughed and applauded. Only then would they have taken up their needles and their thongs, vying with each other to see who could best decorate the living flesh with patterns of beads.

It would have taken a long time. Tanner would have felt it for an eternity. The eyes would have remained, for the squaws would have lost something of their pleasure if their victim had not been able to see what was being done to him. So much of the enjoyment lay in the anticipation.

The fire would have come last. Probably during the night that Herne and the Cavalry were riding towards the Canyon. Dozens and dozens of thin needles of wood inserted in the skin, and then one of the squaws would have waved a blazing torch over the body, igniting them all.

Herne swallowed hard. Turned to the thing hanging at his side, and carefully fired a single shot between where the eyes had once been. The charred object jerked once and then was still. There was surprisingly little blood.

Time to be moving. To follow Emmie-Lou up the steep path, and hope to stay ahead of the Mescalero warriors who would certainly try and regain their captive. And catch the white man who had invaded their camp and butchered their women and children. If they caught Herne, Tanner's sufferings would be nothing compared with what they would do to him.

Jed turned and stepped back into the trees, away from the charred corpse. 'If'n you play with fire, I guess you got to expect to get your fingers burned,' he muttered darkly.

Chapter Seven

The woman was only a little way up the path, sliding back a yard for every two she climbed, her feet slipping in the soft sand. She had lifted up the long dress around her knees to try and make it easier, but the effort was nearly beyond her. Herne caught up with her, pausing only to fully load his Colt again, wishing that he had his Sharps with him. With the accuracy of the long rifle, he could have kept any pursuit safely away from them. But it was a futile thought, and he went back to concentrating on the reality of his situation.

'That dress making it hard?'

'Yes. But I'm not taking it off. I've had enough of being unclothed, Mister . . .? I don't even know your name.'

Her voice was ragged, and Herne realized she was only just holding on to sanity. The horror of what she had seen, and what they must have done to her, followed by the seemingly miraculous rescue had tipped her to the edge of madness. If she cracked up now, he wouldn't be able to carry her. And that would be the best part of nineteen hundred dollars lost.

He decided to be gentle.

'Maybe on the way back home you can tell me some of it. If'n you want to. But right now we got to move out of this arroyo before old One Eye and his brothers come a'gallopin' after us. I'll cut a strip off the bottom of that squaw's dress, and that'll make it a whole lot easier to move up this slope.' He kneeled at her feet, using the bayonet to slice off eighteen inches from the bottom of the deerskin robe.

'I can't do it, Mister . . .?'

'Herne. Jedediah Herne. Your husband hired me to come and get you out of this place.'

'And take me home.'

She infected the word 'home' with a bitter hatred that made Herne look up.

'Have you met Lishe? My husband?'

'Sure. He came to me. Seemed plenty worried about you, Mrs. Parsons. There. That's done. Now we'd best get to climbin' this trail.'

'Did you like my husband?'

'Mrs. Parsons. In a couple of minutes from now, that camp down there is goin' to be brimmin' over with Apaches. And we stand out up here like a dead dog on a dinner table. I'll talk all you like when we're over the top and away, but until then, let's cut it out.'

'I want to know. Have to know, Mister Herne. And I won't move unless . . .'

'Lady! We don't have the time. If I have to I'll bend this gun barrel over your head and carry you.' Herne knew how impossible that would be, but he had to do something.

'Tell me.'

'Right.' Jed was blazingly angry, unable to understand why Emmie-Lou Parsons was behaving this way. 'Your husband, Mrs. Parsons, is not the sort of man I personally would choose if I wanted a fun-filled evening of happy laughter. That answer your question?'

She nodded, raising a hand to push back her tangled hair from off her face. 'Yes. Maybe we can talk a spell when we get out?'

'Maybe. Now . . . Oh! Christ above! Here they come!!'

It may have been the pause in the action from the Cavalry. Or the shooting from behind them. Or one of the squaws could have run to the neck of the Canyon with a warning for One Eye. It didn't matter at all. All that mattered was that there were a half dozen mounted bucks charging along the bottom of the steep-sided valley. All carrying repeating rifles.

And Herne and the woman were still less than half the way up the trail to freedom.

One of Billy Bonney's favourite sayings was: 'There's always a way out. Just a matter of findin' it.' Not that there'd been a way out for Billy the Kid when Pat Garrett dry-gulched him in Pete Maxwell's bedroom in Fort Sumner.

That was just a touch over two years earlier. Jed had heard the news within days of the Kid's death. The best part of a year before his own life was blown apart and his wife died.

Now it looked like his time might be over. If they carried on upwards, then the Apaches could catch them before they got to the top. Furthermore, there were parts of the trail exposed to rifle fire from the Mescalero camp.

'What do we do?' Emmie-Lou Parsons asked plaintively.

'Keep well down. Hands and knees. On the way up you'll find a body or two. Keep on goin'. They'll not concern you. Now git!'

'What about . . .?'

'I'll come up slower, and make them buy the path. And the price is goin' to be damned high.'

He thought she was going to carry on the discussion, but she caught the look in his eyes, and shut her mouth. She had seen that kind of hardness in Lishe's face, and knew it was time to do as she was told. Although the face of her rescuer had the same hardness as her husband, somehow it wasn't as cold or as passionless.

As she scrambled away, keeping as low as she could, the pebbles scraping her knees, Emmie-Lou thought more about the face of Jed Herne.

It was a relief to have her off his back, and he settled down comfortably, with his shoulders against a towering crag, just round one of the twists in the rocky trail, and waited. He knew that the women would have seen which way they went. Short of trying the almost certainly suicidal tactic of hiding somewhere inside the camp, the back entrance was the only place they could have gone.

There was shouting from far beneath him, and several shots cracked out. None of them coming anywhere near enough to cause him any anxiety. From where he rested he could see neither Mrs. Parsons, nor any of the Mescalero braves. He just hoped she didn't show herself. The path opened out over the last twenty feet, and that was the danger point.

His task was to make sure the Apaches were too busy to worry about anyone clawing up that last part of the trail. Two men with rifles, taking their time, could stand in the camp and close off the path. But he guessed that One Eye wouldn't want to do it that way. He'd be blazing angry, wishing to avenge the deaths of the women and the child.

The shooting had stopped. The gunfire from the open mouth of West Wind Canyon had died down to a faltering and irregular crackle. The Cavalry had done what they could, but time had run out.

Although the track wasn't that high, it was steep and treacherous. And narrow enough to stop the Indians coming up it as a bunch. Herne wriggled back so that he was just around the side of the rock, ready to make his move when he was sure the Mescalero hunters were on the straight part immediately beneath him.

As the sun rose higher, he began to sweat. There was a faint breath of wind springing up, and he took off his hat, letting it blow through his greying hair. He stuck out his lower lip and blew air up across his face. Leaning there and waiting. Looking as relaxed as if he was dozing away by the local fishing-hole on a Sabbath afternoon.

But his nerves were taut and ready. He caught the scratch of a foot on the rocks, followed by a muttered word. It was difficult to locate noise up there, bouncing about off the crags and giving false echoes. The sound of men grew louder. If he let them get too close before making a move, they would swamp him. Better to move too soon.

'Hell!'

Too soon.

The Canyon had tricked him. Although his ears had told him the chasing Apaches were nearly on top of him, they were still a whole bend of the path away. The first of them had only just taken the first cautious step into sight, looking back to tell the others the way was clear.

Herne's bullet told them different, hitting the brave in the left shoulder, sending him three steps back, dropping his gun, arms flailing. He had only been two steps from the edge of the drop, and disappeared over it with a great cry of pain and shock and anger. A cry that was only stopped by the wet thump of his body hitting the rocks below.

A rifle appeared around the turn of the path, and five shots blazed away in Jed's general direction. But by then he was safely out of sight behind the crag, already scuttling up the next straight bit to further cover.

'We will catch you, killer of babies!'

'Stealer of women and burner of helpless prisoners! You are a running dog who fears his shadow.'

'I will kill you, white eyes!!'

'Then come and do it. Or go back to the wickiups and tend to your squaws. They are braver than cowardly One Eye!'

While he spoke, Herne had ejected the spent cartridge, ramming home a fresh round. Spinning the chamber to make sure he had the full six rounds. It was habit to check, though he was so used to the weight of the Colt that he could have told if someone had filed a quarter inch off one of the bullets.

'You will not run free. When we have you we run down the white woman and I will teach her about running from me.'

'Seems everyone wants to stop Mrs. Parsons running away from them,' commented Jed to himself.

A shower of small pebbles cascaded from high above him, telling him that Emmie-Lou must be close to the top. And that thought reminded him that the body of the third of the sentries he'd killed must be close to where he was. If his memory was right the corpse would be starting to stiffen up on the next twist of the trail.

He reached around his cover and fired two quick shots, making a dash along one of the more open parts of the path to the next bend. A ragged volley of shots followed him, one of them spitting splinters of stone within a yard of his right hand. Then he collapsed, panting with the effort of the steep climb, and reloaded yet again. There was always the temptation during a break in the action to sit back and gather breath. First things had to be done first. And the very first of all was to keep a fully loaded gun.

The body was still where he'd left it, though a light film of dust lay across it where Emmie-Lou had scrambled by. Herne sat and looked at it, and grinned.

'Only useful Indian around here is going to be you.'

There were five of the Mescalero braves left alive, including their chief, One Eye. The way Herne figured it, there was only one way of making sure that he and Emmie-Lou Parsons got away clean, and that was to kill all of them. And if that wasn't possible, then he had to try and get them off his back.

The body of the man he had killed half-way down the

trail was only slightly stiff, sprawled forwards on its face, the pool of blood crimson at its centre, and darkening to brown at the edges as it began to congeal. Both chest and back were heavily stained with drying blood, but that didn't make his plan impossible. Waving away the insects that were eagerly lapping at the feast, Jed heaved the corpse to its feet, and dragged it awkwardly to the boulder that blocked off the turning of the trail. Propping it against himself, draping the limp arms on his own shoulders. Held it round the neck with his left hand, keeping the right free for the Colt. Then all there was to do was wait and listen.

Below, One Eye was leading his men, urging them to keep silent in their pursuit of this dog who had killed half a dozen of their women while the pony-soldiers in blue kept them pinned down at the entrance to West Wind Canyon. But they had made the Cavalry pay for their feint. The young officer with them had brought them in too close so that some of the Mescalero sharp-shooters were able to get above them, and fire down over the top of their meagre cover. Killing, One Eye reckoned, at least eight or nine.

So that meant that it had been equal. Though the white man they stalked now must have disposed of at least two sentries to sneak in the way that he had. One Eye wanted him in his hands, and he also wanted the white woman back. He was conscious of the instant swelling at the front of his cotton trousers at the memory of the pleasure that he had taken of her. He and all of the other warriors.

Though she had laid passive and still at the beginning, her nature had betrayed her. They had held her still. Easily with their greater strength and numbers. Braves took it in turns to stand across her wrists, while others each held a leg, forcing her thighs wide apart, to ease the entrance for their brothers. Yet after seven of them had spent their lust in her, the woman had begun to roll and kick and cry out. At first in anger. But later she had cried out and the Mescalero men had laughed for they knew that it was no longer anger, but a need to be taken and taken brutally and often.

One Eye wished that he had her there, between his legs, so that he could ride out his hatred of the white race on her. But first there was this lone man to take. The path would be too steep for him to move fast without being heard. Perhaps he was waiting around the next bend.

'Aaaargh! No! Help!! Help!'

The Mescalero chief looked round at his brothers, wondering what the cry meant. Could one of the sentries have sneaked up from the top of the Canyon and surprised the dog?

'Red Wolf. Take care and look around the twist of the path and see what happens. Beware in case the white man tries to fool us.'

The Apache named by his chief crawled to the front of the party, his necklace of wolf's teeth rattling as he moved. He stuck his head around the rocks and stared up the trail.

'Damn you! Son of a . . .! Noooo!!'

'It is Lost Pony. He has taken the cur from behind and they struggle. Come!'

'Wait,' said One Eye, suspicious of a trap.

'No!' shouted Red Wolf, standing up. 'We must help him or all is lost. Forward brothers to aid Lost Pony.'

'No,' said One Eye, but it is not easy for an Apache chief to stop his warriors once the desire for blood-letting clouds their minds. He was brushed aside. When he stepped more cautiously around the corner, he saw his four men scrambling on hands and knees up the steep incline.

At the top of it, half-masked by one of the huge red boulders, he saw the cursed white man, and indeed he was locked in a death struggle with Lost Pony. They rocked backwards and forwards, holding each other tightly. There was no sign of the woman, but she could not have gone far. His men were only ten paces away, and yet still some doubt nagged at One Eye's mind, like the worm in a ripe peach.

What was wrong?

'Wait!' Of course. Lost Pony had gone up from the camp to relieve the other sentries. They had not raised an alarm, so they must be dead. If they were dead, then Lost Pony would have been climbing the face of the cliff at the same time that the white man was climbing down. Even in the dim light of early morning it would not have been humanly possible for them to have passed without his brother seeing the intruder. So Lost Pony could not be fighting the white man. He must be . . .

'He is dead!!' he screamed, seeing his doubt made a certainty as the enemy swung Lost Pony to cover himself, and they could all see the dreadful hole in his back, stained dark with his life-blood.

'No!' yelled Red Wolf, now within reaching distance of the couple. His rifle was still held low in his hand as he climbed up, not wishing to fire earlier for fear of hitting Lost Pony. And now it was too late. On the narrow path all was confusion as the four Apaches tried to escape.

Herne's bullets were too quick for them. Firing under the dangling arm of the Mescalero corpse, he was able to steady himself and gun them down with no risk and no difficulty. It needed five bullets to take out the four warriors.

Red Wolf was hit in the side of the head, just below the bright blue headband, the bullet puddling his brains to pulp.

As he fell the second man was exposed, and he died in the same way, his skull shattered by a single shot. He dropped, and the third man tried to hide behind him. Jed's shot took him narrowly through the very top of the head, the bullet splintering a section of the cranium and exiting upwards. It knocked him out, but failed to kill him.

Behind him, the fourth man was already on his way back down the slippery path, his rifle left behind in his blind panic to escape. Herne took steady aim, and shot him through the back of the neck, toppling him on his face, blood pouring from his throat, and from his mouth. He rolled and slid all the way down to where One Eye stood paralysed by the sudden horror of his men's death, landing sightlessly at his chief's feet.

The Mescalero levered at the Winchester like a man in a frenzy, sending a half dozen shots upwards at the single man who had decimated his small tribe. Three of them smacked into the protecting corpse of Lost Pony, hitting the body with a dull, soggy thud, their impact absorbed by the dead flesh.

The man shot through the top of the head rolled over, trying to claw his way to his feet, feeling with one hand at the gaping wound that had streaked his long hair with blood. His last thought before Herne shot him through the face was that he had been lucky not to have been killed. The corpse flopped back on top of the other two.

Herne dropped the body of Lost Pony and jumped back out of sight round the corner, bumping into a terrified Emmie-Lou Parsons.

'What the Hell . . .?'

'I heard you call, and I thought . . . Oh God, I thought you were dead.'

The girl flung herself at him, sobbing uncontrollably, clinging to him with the strength of someone drowning. Her arms were round his neck, pinning his gun-hand to his side, making it impossible for him to reload. Even at that moment of heightened danger, Jed was aware that the woman was naked under the stinking robe, and that her breasts were young and firm, pressing against his chest.

He didn't think that it was possible for any man to come up that treacherous path silently and at speed. But One Eye was a man possessed of a blind rage, stoked with a burning disbelief that this thing could have happened. In one hour of one morning everything had gone.

Before this white eyes came to his camp, he had been leader of a small tribe. But a secure tribe. Feared and respected throughout the Sierra Mogollon, and untouchable thanks to their hide-out in West Wind Canyon. Their name had been raised even more by the capture of the lovely wife of Elisha Parsons. Man with Eyes of Snake and Heart of Stone. That was the Apache name for him.

Now a whole hand and three of his finest warriors were dead. A hand of the squaws, and one child. With his depleted force he could no longer hope to hold the Canyon. They were lost, and would become a homeless sub-tribe, driven to living close to a larger group, depending on them for comfort, for defence and for food.

And that had sent him mad, his brain filled with only one desire. To kill this white man, regardless of the risk to himself. And so One Eye had run up the sheer path, ignoring the dizzy drop to his left, his rifle clutched in his hand, stepping lightly and unbelievably fast.

Never expecting to find his prey so delivered up to him, helplessly tangled in the arms of the white woman who wore the deerskin robe of one of his murdered squaws. His lips peeled back from his teeth in a feral snarl of pleasure as he brought the Winchester up to his hip, levering a round into the chamber, and cocking the hammer with his thumb.

Herne saw the Mescalero appear almost out of the living rock. He faced a mask of insane hatred. So close that he was able to see that the name of One Eye was correct in its way. Though the chief had two eyes, they were indeed of different colours. The right one blue and the left one brown, giving his face a bizarre skewed appearance.

Gripped by the weeping Emmie-Lou, Jed hadn't got a whole lot of options open to him. He brought his knee up sharply, feeling it grate against the girl's pubic bone, sending her retching away from him, hands clutched at her groin. Herne followed that act of chivalry by swinging left-handed at her, catching her high across the left cheek, knocking her away from him to her hands and knees, bouncing heavily against the rough cliff wall.

One Eye saw the one target suddenly become two, and the barrel of the Winchester wavered uncertainly. His finger squeezed the trigger, propelled by simple hatred rather than by any controlled motive. The bullet exploded across the couple of paces, splintering red shards of rock across the winding trail.

Clean between the two whites, missing them both.

'Die!' screamed the Mescalero, levering a second round and aiming at Herne.

'Die yourself,' said Herne, having had the time to draw the Colt from the holster and cock and aim.

It was his last round.

It was also the last round in One Eye's Winchester.

Herne fired his last round.

The Apache didn't.

The heavy calibre bullet was perfectly aimed, drilling through the left eye. The brown eye. Burying itself in the brain. The impact sending the Mescalero toppling backwards, his feet scraping, fingers clawing at the warm morning air in a dying effort to keep from falling to the jagged rocks nearly a hundred feet below.

Death came before he could regain his balance, and he vanished from the path. Herne ignored the sobbing woman and looked down over the brink to where the body of the Apache lay smashed and broken. Even from that height, Herne could see the one eye gazing vacantly back at him, the other socket a dark blood-filled pit.

'Good name for you, One Eye,' he said. 'Now you really earned it.'

Chapter Eight

'Mister Herne?'

Emmie-Lou kept trying.

'Mister Herne?'

'My name's Jed.'

'All right. Jed?'

'What is it, Mrs. Parsons?'

'My name's Emmie-Lou. If I call you Jed, then why won't you call me that?'

'I'm employed by your husband, Mrs. Parsons. I wouldn't want to get familiar with the wife of the man who's paying me two and one half thousand dollars.'

'That much?'

'Yeah. That much.'

The horse jogged easily on, towards the Fort. Herne had taken her slowly down the path through the Devil's Playground, knowing that the death of One Eye would mean the end to any direct pursuit. But he had no wish to risk being caught out in the open by any vengeful mounted party of young bucks, so he had taken a slow detour away from the Canyon, coming towards Fort Gilman near sundown.

Twice Emmie-Lou Parsons had fallen asleep, until he had run a rope around her, fastening her behind him in the saddle. And twice she had begun to ask him not to take her back. But his response had silenced her.

For the time.

'Nearly there. Rest the night, and set off towards your spread first light tomorrow. Get a mount for you from the Cavalry. Guess that this time tomorrow and you'll be back with Mister Parsons.'

'And you'll have done your job and got your blood money, Mister Herne.'

'Yes, ma'am. Not your blood on the money.'

'From what I've seen, I doubt it would have worried you if it had been.'

'Deal was alive or proven dead. If you'd been dead, I'd have found a way of telling your old man 'bout it.'

'Truly that much money?'

'Two and a half thousand dollars American. That's what he reckons you're worth.'

She was quiet, though he could feel her arms still tight around his waist. When they got to Fort Gilman one of his first priorities would be a hot bath. Rid himself of the stink of gunplay. Blood and death. And the smell of the grease on the woman's borrowed dress.

'You're wonderin' how much it might take to buy me off so you can carry on runnin'. Reckonin' if you had, say, three thousand dollars, that would buy your freedom?'

Emmie-Lou didn't reply.

'That's right, isn't it, Mrs. Parsons?'

'Maybe.'

'I'll set your mind to ease. If you had it, which you don't, it wouldn't make no difference to me. I've got me a good contract to return you home, Mrs. Parsons. I'll have done my part by sun-down tomorrow. I'll collect my bounty, and ride on. Anything happens after that's between you and your husband.'

'You don't know Lishe!' The note of desperation was hardly veiled.

'Nope. Then again, Mrs. Parsons, I'm not the one as married him.'

'Please. Jed. I'm so grateful for what you did for me. Saving me from those fiends.'

'It's a job, Ma'am. Just another job.'

'But didn't it mean anything to you that a white woman was being . . . being . . .'

'I know damned well what you was being, Mrs. Parsons. I always did hear that when it was inevitable, you ought to just lie back and enjoy it.'

As soon as the bitter words were out of his mouth he regretted them. Thinking back to the seven men who'd raped and brutally abused his lovely young wife. She'd not lain back and enjoyed it. Nor had Becky's Ma. She'd lost her life trying to protect herself from a fate that some said was worse.

'You are a first line bastard, Mister Herne. I see now why Lishe hired you. You and he are alike. Cast from the same mold of ice.'

'You're wrong, Mrs. Parsons. And I'm sorry for what I said. It was foolish. I apologize for it. And the reason that your husband hired me rather than any other bounty gunman is that I'm the best.'

Emmie-Lou was a little mollified by the apology, but still angry and upset. 'And the modesty goes with the job, I suppose, Mister Herne?'

'You kill as many as I have, Mrs. Parsons, and you get to know that modesty is a luxury that only the second-best can afford.'

'They did awful things to me. You want to hear about them, Jed?'

Emmie-Lou had decided that there could be only two possible ways of avoiding being taken home. One was to kill the tall, middle-aged man who had just plucked her from the middle of a closely-guarded Apache camp. The second alternative was to seduce him away from his duty.

'My breasts are so sore and bruised from the way they came at me. Did you see them?'

'Yes. Yes, I saw them, Mrs. Parsons, and I'm right sorry for you.'

'They are so bruised and painful. What they need is a gentle massage. If you weren't a stranger to me, I might ask you if . . .' she laughed, tightening her arms about his middle. 'I guess you've seen more of me than any man, 'cept Lishe, of course.'

Jed made no answer, guiding the tired horse towards the distant specks of light that were Fort Gilman, wondering when Emmie-Lou would stop bothering. But she had a Hell of a fine figure, and it had been a long time since . . . A long time since anything.

'I'm rubbing them better now. Holding on with my left hand to your broad back, while I touch my bosom with my right hand. There.' She sighed, and the fingers of her left tightened on the back of his shirt, digging into his back. 'Oh, that feels so very good. They're really painful, Jed, but just running the tips of my fingers around the ends of them makes them stand out and feel so grand.'

'Mrs. Parsons, I'd be telling lies if I said that I didn't find you an attractive woman. And you talkin' like that gets me all heated up, just like it would any man who hadn't been gelded.'

'I can be taken by the right man, Jed. I want you to know that.'

'That's clearer than a bullet in the guts, but I want you to know what I think, Mrs. Parsons.'

'What's that, Jed?'

'The right man who can have you is your husband. I don't know why you married him, and I don't rightly care. But you're wed to him, and as long as you are, then you don't have the right to go offerin' yourself to me as a bribe to try and get away free.'

'*I* don't have the right! *You* don't have the right to tell me that. You don't understand what I've been through! He doesn't have the right to do the wrong that he's done to me '.

'Maybe. I guess that knowin' don't make it any easier to lose out, Mrs. Parsons. But I'm takin' you back to your home at sun-up tomorrow. You walk in through the front door of that house, and I collect. After that you can go where you like and I won't give a damn.'

'He won't let me go again. He swore after last time what would happen. Said that he'd chain me and . . .'

Herne tugged savagely at the reins, pulling the horse up short with a whinny of protest. Eased himself forward in the saddle and looked back at Emmie-Lou over his shoulder. Closing his mind to the fact that the squaw's dress was pulled open clear down the front and her fingers capped her right breast, making the nipple stand out blood-red against the white of her soft skin.

'You stop that or I'll tie your wrists behind your back! I've had enough of your damned whining. I don't want a damned medal for what I done. I just want my dollars. And by God, Mrs. Parsons, I will collect them! I don't want one more word out of you until we reach the Fort. That'll be around a quarter of an hour. So hold off on the noise!'

Her hand dropped from her breast, and she laced up the greasy dress to the neck, finding that her fingers were trembling. As they walked on towards the swelling shadow of Fort Gilman, she wondered about the next day. It was a long, hard ride to the spread. And Herne had admitted that he found her attractive.

It wasn't over yet.

Lieutenant Pinner was waiting for them just inside the heavy gates, his face pale and anxious in the light of the torches. Beyond him, on the edge of the parade-ground, Jed saw a party of troopers on their hands and knees, working backwards towards the edges of the square, each with a small brush in his hand, smoothing the sand to a perfect finish.

'Major still getting his priorities in the right order, I see,' he said, reining in by the young officer. 'Oh, and this is Mrs. Parsons, who is tired and needs a bath. Get a couple of women to look after her.'

Emmie-Lou hadn't spoken a word since his angry warning, and allowed Pinner to help her from the horse. Despite her fatigue she couldn't help noticing his look of surprise at what she was wearing. And the fact that she was so obviously naked underneath it.

'Lady's had a bad time, Lieutenant. Want her fresh and rested to be away before first light in the morning. Get a trooper to take care of my horse, and arrange a fresh mount for her for tomorrow. Want to be away from the Parsons' spread before sundown.'

Pinner gave the necessary orders, escorting Emmie-Lou to the married quarters, where a brood of fluttering women came clucking out to help her. Jed stood by his horse waiting for the young officer to return, suddenly feeling bone-weary. He drew the Sharps from its bucket and hefted it over his shoulders. His mount was walked away by a trooper towards the livery stables.

Pinner returned and stood in front of him, biting his lip. Absently making patterns in the sand with the toe of his boot.

'What's wrong, boy? I was there on time. You were there on time. I got out the woman. The ramrod . . . what was his name?'

'Tanner.'

'Yeah. Tanner, had been worked over by the Mescalero women for two or three days, so there wasn't much I could do for him.'

'Was he still alive?'

Herne shook his head. 'Not when I left he wasn't.'

'Major said he wanted to see you as soon as you got back. If you got back.'

'I'm having me a bath first. And a few cups of some good strong coffee. Thick enough to float a Dragoon Colt on the top. *Then* maybe I'll see the Major.'

'It's an Army Fort, Herne. He can make you.'

There was something wrong. The Lieutenant was nervous and on edge. The former deferential politeness gone.

'Sorry, son. Guess I didn't hear you too good. You seemed to be sayin' something 'bout draggin' me along right now to see the Major. Can't be right, can it? Less you want to be the man to start draggin'?'

He shifted the long rifle to his left hand and took a half-step back from the officer, letting his right hand fall, *very* casually, to hover a couple of inches over the butt of the Colt. It was done so easily and naturally that anyone standing five yards away would have seen nothing to it. But Pinner read the message loud and clear.

'Very well. I have done what Major Corwin ordered, and if you choose to ignore that order there is nothing short of force that I can do.'

'Not ignoring it, son. Just sort of delaying it a while. Go and tell Major Corwin I'll be with him within the hour.'

Pinner turned on his heel and began to march away, halting when Herne called after him. 'You want to tell me what's wrong, or do I wait for the Major?'

Uncertainly, the young officer eyed him, his face a white blur in the evening dimness. 'I ... he's very angry. Very angry indeed.'

'Someone fart on guard duty?'

'No. The raid today ... There were heavy losses.'

'Heavy ...!'

'And you didn't fire the camp like you promised to do on the way out.'

'Well ... That's ...' Jed rubbed his nose, using time to

control his own anger. 'I guess that maybe I'd better hear all this from the man himself. No point in you and me fallin' out over it, and then havin' to do it all over again with the Major.'

Pinner saluted him and marched away without another word, and Jed went to have his bath. Wondering what could have gone that wrong.

The water was wonderfully warm, and Jed had nearly fallen asleep, stretched out there in the tin bath. One of the troopers had brought in the coffee, and Herne had asked him about the mission that day.

'Not my affair, sir. All I know is that there was a lot of good men killed, and they say that it was down to you that we didn't wipe out the bastards. Beggin' your pardon, sir, but you asked me.'

After he'd gone, Jed dressed slowly, wondering how the Cavalry had lost men in what was supposed to be a routine engage and hold operation. No doubt Major Corwin would be more than happy to tell him how it had happened.

Before going over to the Major's quarters, carefully avoiding the sacred square, Herne looked in on the married quarters to see how Mrs. Parsons was. There too he was greeted with a mixture of active dislike and cold formality.

'The poor wee chick's sleeping like a babe after all the dreadful things she's been through. And she doesn't need you here, Mister Herne the Hunter. We know about you.'

'What do you know?'

'That where you step flowers die. That you're something a mite lower than a rattler. And that there are three women here widows because of you. And five mothers'll be mourning their sons as well, soon as they get the regulation messages. Good night to you.'

He'd walked away from the angry little Irish woman, wife

to the farrier, and gone to Corwin's office, the cold rage inside him heating to the point of violence. If someone had blundered, then he was damned if he was going to be the one to carry home the blame like a dead buzzard strapped around his shoulders.

The door was partly open, so he pushed it wide and walked in. Corwin was sitting down behind his desk working on a detailed plan with coloured pencils. He jumped like a shot jack-rabbit at Herne's appearance, his small red face swollen with self-righteous indignation.

'Don't you have the manners to knock on a door before entering?'

'When I'm *ordered* to attend like I was, then I figure that manners don't figure in things. You busy workin' out a new way of polishin' door handles?' pointing to the plan on the officer's desk.

'No. No, this is . . . the routine for the sentries' duties now you have raised the South-West against us.'

'You're a whole barrel of laughs, Major. Come on. Let's get this load of bull-shit over with. I'm tired and I want to get off your Fort as soon as possible in the morning.'

'And I shall be glad to see you leave, Mister Herne. Sentry!! Sentry!!'

'Sir?'

'Officers' call. Here and now. And I do mean *now*!'

While they waited, neither of them spoke. Herne hooked himself a chair and sat down, making sure his back was to a corner and he faced the door. Not that he really thought he was in any danger. It was just a habit. A way of cutting chances and living a while longer.

Within a couple of minutes the entire officer complement of Fort Gilman was there. Two Captains and three Lieutenants, including young Pinner. The last of them to arrive snatched a glance at the detailed colours on the plan on Major Corwin's desk.

'Nearly completed the rota for collecting more stones to edge all the paths, sir?' he asked in an interested voice.

'No. That's not ... I'll talk later about that. Please find a place to sit or lean, gentlemen.'

'Sure you can take the time off from your ... sentry duties, Major?' asked Herne with a broad grin, pleased to see the increasing discomfiture of the plump officer.

'I have asked you all here as witnesses while I talk to this man. He came here asking our help in rescuing the wife of Elisha Parsons, taken by One Eye's men.'

'A lady that you were prepared to leave in West Wind Canyon to rot, Major. Leaving her to the Apaches to rape as and when they wanted. Ask her what it was like. She'll tell you about life in West Wind Canyon.'

'Do not interrupt. I arranged for a large patrol under Lieutenant Pinner to accompany Mister Herne there and give him covering fire while he went in alone. That being the plan that offered most hope of success. In return, he agreed to start a fire in the camp in the hope of helping to abbreviate the stay of One Eye and his troublesome warriors. That was the deal.'

'Forgive me, Major Corwin, but that's not quite right. Near to it, but missin' a detail here and there. Way I hear it, One Eye and his bucks have been there for months, and you've done damn-all to blast him out. And I didn't agree to burn any of his wickiups, which don't burn anyway. I just went in for the lady.'

'That was all you get paid for, Mister Herne?' asked a sour-faced, grizzled Captain.

'Right. Way I see it, I done you a Hell of a good turn today.'

'Eight troopers were killed and several more wounded! Is that your help?'

Herne had been doing a spell of thinking about the losses,

and was reasonably sure he'd come up with the answer. He looked across the room at young Pinner.

'Tell me about the deaths, Lieutenant. How you figure they was down to me?'

'Well . . . I arrived as we agreed, and placed my men in a wide circle around the entrance to the Canyon. We had arrived without being seen. At fifteen minutes after five, at the time decided, we opened heavy and concentrated fire. In time they came and returned the fire.'

'How many?'

'Couple of dozen. One Eye has only that many braves.'

'Your losses?' asked Herne with deceptive gentleness. 'How do you lose that many?'

'I was waiting for you to fire the place before making my withdrawal. To give you the best chance I could to rescue the lady.'

'Damn noble. Except that you knew that there wouldn't be a fire. We talked about it last night.'

Corwin stood up, pointing at Herne. 'That's a lie, Mister. I'll have you . . .'

'Have me what, Major? Painting your stones? Or polishing your parade-ground so it gleams?'

'I . . . I waited as long as possible, and that gave some of the Mescalero braves a chance to get high up the cliffs and direct their fire downwards. That was how the losses came.'

Pinner was lying. Herne knew it.

'Lieutenant Pinner?'

The young man looked across the room at him, uncertainty in his face. 'Yes?'

'From the top of the back entrance it's possible from one spot to see the mouth of the Canyon where your men were placed. Did you know that?'

'No. No I didn't.'

Jed was about to gamble. 'I saw where you'd put your

troopers. You want to tell the Major how far from the Canyon you'd put them?'

'Far enough.'

'How far's that?'

Pinner was silent. Major Corwin looked from his face to Herne and back again, unable to understand what was going on.

Herne ignored the other men, speaking directly to the young officer. 'You told me something Nathan Brittles used to say, about apologizing. He also used to say that it was a big man that made no mistakes. And a bigger one who admitted it when he made one. Better you tell them, son.'

Pinner cleared his throat, pulling himself up to stand at attention. 'Mister Herne is correct, sir. I regret to say that I brought my men in too close. Within a hundred yards of the hostile Indians. They could easily climb and fire over our cover. Which they did. I never thought of it as it was dark when we took up positions.'

'You friggin' young . . .! I would have thought that any wet-eared puppy would have been more careful!'

Herne interrupted him. 'I would have thought Major Corwin that any officer worthy of the name would not have delegated such an important mission to an inexperienced officer. Most Commanding Officers would have done it themselves!'

Corwin looked as though he might explode. 'Damn your nerve, Herne! I was otherwise engaged this morning, or I would have been there. And if you make suggestions of cowardice, then I think you owe me an instant apology. I was not the one who sneaked in behind the corpses of my brave men and came running out again, carrying a naked bitch who should have known better than to get herself caught. You have done nothing but run like the braggart you are. A braggart and a stinkin' coward!!'

For a moment, like glass beads on a curtain, the words

hung suspended in the space of the crowded hot office. Herne had known many men in his life who would have reached for their guns at words like those. And murdered the stubby Major in hot blood.

The temptation was there. He felt it surge through him like a flood tide, but he checked it. Pleasant though it would be to put a bullet through that crimson turkey-face, the other men were all carrying side-arms. He couldn't kill them all.

Slowly, so there wouldn't be any misunderstanding, Jed rose from his seat, taking care to keep both hands well away from the Colt. Took the two steps that brought him face to face with Corwin, and lashed him open-handed across the mouth, knocking him back in his chair with the force of the blow.

'No coward, Major,' he said, stepping back instantly, so that the officers moving in to restrain him found themselves foolishly stranded in mid-stride. Corwin sat still, the colour driven from his cheeks, apart from the weals of Herne's fingers scarlet on his skin. The power of the slap had caught the side of his nose and a thin trickle of blood ran down, splashing on the neat little plan.

'I'll . . . I'll . . . have you . . .'

'Nothing.' Jed sat down again, looking round the office, meeting the eyes of every man there and holding each glance until the other looked away. 'All these men know you for a fool. A liar. A braggart. An inefficient petty coward. Every man at Fort Gilman must know that. And if they don't, then I'll find a way of tellin' them before I leave.'

'If it weren't for my rank I would call you out for that,' blustered Corwin.

Pinner interrupted him. 'Beg your pardon, sir, but I don't recall any specific bar on an affair of honour for a man of your rank. Not for such a great insult.'

If looks could have slain, Pinner would have slumped

dead on the floor. 'Thank you very much, Lieutenant. I shall not forget that.'

'You won't fight me?'

'No.' Corwin looked down at his desk, seeing the blood and reaching for a linen handkerchief to try and staunch the flow. Ignoring everyone else in the room.

'That's all, then. I'll leave you. Make sure all's ready for me before dawn, would you, son?'

Pinner nodded, half-smiling at the tall man. 'I'll see to it, Mister Herne. Thanks a lot.'

As he reached the door, Herne paused, looking back at the frozen, uncomfortable tableau of officers. 'One other thing, gentlemen. I guess you'll have no more trouble with One Eye. Send out a patrol tomorrow to West Wind Canyon, maybe under Lieutenant Pinner. Nobody's goin' to be there to stop you taking the place.'

'Why?' It was the grey-haired Captain. A man close to Herne's own age.

'While I was gettin' the lady out, I found time to send nine of the Mescalero braves to their happy huntin' ground.'

'Nine!'

'Including One Eye himself. Good night, gentlemen.'

He closed the door firmly behind him, then paused on the wooden verandah, waiting to hear what happened in the Major's office after his departure. He stood there for a full two minutes, and there was nothing. Not a sound.

A long empty silence.

Herne went for a walk around the compound before turning in for the night, to clear his head and get some fresh air after the sweaty confines of Corwin's office. Nobody came to speak to him, and he finally walked back towards his own hut at around midnight.

There was a note under the door. Unsigned, but he

guessed it was from young Pinner. 'Even a coward can arrange a killing. If a sentry saw someone leaving around dawn, and he'd been told it might be an Apache stealing a horse, then a bullet in the back would clear a lot of things. Make sure you're away by five when there's a guard change. Please burn this.'

Herne sat there for four or five minutes, trying to decide what to do. It wouldn't be that hard to go quietly across and kill Corwin. Slit his throat and make it look as if an Apache really had got into Fort Gilman. But maybe it would be better to let him stay alive. Make him look the damned fool he was.

A grin crawled on to Jed's face, and stayed there.

Before turning in he took the metal dish that had held a scanty supper of bread and beans, and placed the note on it. Lighting it and watching it smoke away to a blackened wisp so light that he was able to blow it to the floor and crush it under his boot-heel. Then he took off his shirt and loosened his belt, climbing on the bunk, making sure that his Colt hung on the nail by the head of the bed, turned so that the butt was ready to his hand.

He would need to wake around three, he decided.

It was just before ten to three when he blinked awake, checking that the shutters were across the windows before lighting the smoky lamp. Tugging on his shirt and buckling on the heavy gun-belt. Stepping quietly to the door and peering out across the sleeping Fort. The sentries paced their regular beat along the cat-walks, pausing every now and again to stare out over the barren, empty land.

'Leaving, Mister Herne?'

'Right, Mister Pinner. And my name's Jed to those I number among friends.'

'And my name's Cyrus. Like my Pa. I want you to know, Jed, that I'm not shamed by my Pa. Sure he did a lot of things that weren't by the book, but he did what he thought he had to, and that's not a bad code for a man to live by.'

Herne could have stopped to argue that one through, but it wasn't the time or the place. He stepped into the pool of darkness under the slope of the roof and whispered for a few moments to the young officer, who began to laugh. So amused that he had to bite his sleeve to bring himself under control.

'Terrific. You kicked him in the gut in that office and showed him up for what he is. That'll really finish him as far as Fort Gilman is concerned.'

'Maybe as far as the U.S. Cavalry is concerned, as well,' said Herne. 'Now let's go. I'll get the horses and what I need from the stables, and you get Mrs. Parsons.'

'I know where she is and I can get to her without anyone else seeing.'

'Fine. No need for you to get dragged into all this. What about the sentry?'

'Sergeant Quincannon's on the gate until five. Good man. Hates Corwin's guts like poison. He'll let you and the lady through and swear blind he didn't see nothing wrong.'

'And the paint?'

'Got the key to the stores. I'll bring it out for you.'

Pinner began to move away, when Herne called him back. 'Best you do what we said, and then get back to your bed. Sleep tight and wake late. That way there won't be a thing that Corwin can do to link you with what'll have happened. And, thanks a lot, Cyrus. Good luck.'

The Lieutenant shook his hand firmly, and vanished off into the blackness. The last Herne heard was his voice, floating in from beyond the hut. 'Take care not to step on the Major's parade-ground. You know how touchy he is about that.'

And a faint laugh.

* * *

'Why we have to creep away like this?'

Emmie-Lou's voice had the rasping, querulous tone of someone wakened too early. Herne stepped in close and put his hand over her mouth.

'Because I say so, and that's all. Now keep your mouth shut until we're clear and away from here. Understood?'

She reached up and moved his hand. 'Yes. That's very clear, Jed. If you want to get me back even earlier and get your money an hour sooner, that's your concern. I shan't speak another word.'

Herne nodded sourly. 'Startin' now. Mount up.'

The Fort had provided a bay mare for her, and his own stallion had been watered and fed. The Squaw's dress had disappeared and had been replaced with a sensible long skirt and blouse in dark blue. The property of the wife of a doctor who had come to the South-West fresh from qualifying back in Boston the previous month. And had both died of cholera within a week of their arrival. Her blistered feet wore the riding boots that the same lady had brought two thousand miles in her baggage, and had never worn.

'Wait here. I'll be about five minutes. Got a visit to make to the stables, and a mite of writin' to do. Then we'll move.'

Emmie-Lou sat the mare in the blackness, the only noise the patrolling boots of the sentries, and the occasional snicker from the horses. The sliver of moon was hidden by shreds of cloud racing across it, giving only the palest of glows. The parade-ground was a perfect, immaculate square. For a moment she thought that she saw someone moving on it, but when she stared hard, there was nobody there.

The blackness and the cold made her think of the home that she would be seeing tomorrow. No, it was already today. There was only the long ride across the bleak land through the heat and sun towards the Parsons' spread. Lishe would greet her, and pay off Herne the Hunter. And he'd ride away after his next damned bounty, and the door would close. She felt tears flooding her eyes and wiped them away with the sleeve of the blue blouse.

It was so unfair. She had less than a day to try and persuade the grim-faced gunman to change his mind, and she knew with a bitter heart that there wasn't a lot of chance of that. But she'd sure try.

Minutes dragged past, and then Herne was back at her side, swinging easily up in the high saddle. She smelled an odd mixture of manure and paint, but didn't question him. She knew enough from her marriage that the age of chivalry existed only in books. Lishe had shown her that too many times.

'We ride. Come on.'

'But that's across . . .'

He touched her arm, and she winced at the power in the grip. 'Remember what you said. Ride where I say and keep your lips well buttoned. I know what I'm doin'.'

The torch at the gate showed them the way out, and they rode silently past the saluting figure of Sergeant Quincannon. His massive figure straight as a ramrod, his battered face creased in a smile. Herne nodded to him as they rode through the open gateway. Hearing it creak closed behind them as they headed away east.

The shock killed Corwin.

He already suffered from very high blood-pressure, and the horror that greeted him when he was called from his bed just after sunup was too much for him. The blood pumped through his body too fast. His face grew redder and more swollen. His fingers tore at his collar, and froth hung at the corners of his mouth. Purple veins sprang out across his forehead, and his eyes rolled in their sockets.

With a piercing scream of inarticulate rage, the little Major spun about like a child's top, and fell to the packed earth, landing on his face with a noise like a rotten apple breaking.

He was dead by the time they got him to his quarters, though there was no doctor there to certify him. It fell to the farrier, as an expert in animals, and the two senior officers to write that their Commanding Officer had died from: 'A falling fit, brought on by a shock.'

Everyone knew who'd done the dreadful deed, but nobody ever mentioned the name of Herne. Pinner got his transfer, and Fort Gilman became a tight-knit fighting establishment. Within two days West Wind Canyon had been cleared of the shattered remnants of One Eye's band, and the narrow entrance closed for ever with dynamite.

Knowing Corwin's fanatical devotion to his parade-ground, it was the obvious place for a gesture of revenge. When Corwin came out into the orange-pink morning sunlight, he saw that its smooth, immaculate surface was torn up by hoof-marks, as though a pair of horses had been trotted repeatedly backwards and forwards over it.

And right in the centre of it was a pile of manure, carried from the stables in a couple of buckets, neatly heaped into a miniature pyramid. Protruding from the middle of the heap was a pole. The handle of a broom, with a piece of paper tacked to it. It was the writing on this paper that toppled Major Corwin from anger to fatal apoplexy.

It said: 'Question: What is the connection between this pile and the orders of the cowardly Major Corwin? Answer: They both come from a horse's ass.'

It wasn't signed, but it didn't really need to be. From then on in Fort Gilman was a corner-stone in the continuing legend of Herne the Hunter.

Chapter Nine

The sun was baking the land, pushing the temperature well over the hundred mark. It bounced back off the rocks and sand, roasting the two riders as they slowly made their way away from the Sierra Mogollon towards the centre of Parsons' spread. It made the stock of the Sharps rifle burning hot. Danced off the small golden ear-rings that Emmie-Lou wore. Herne had noticed them before, and had been surprised that the Apaches hadn't ripped them off. Then he'd recalled that her hair had been long and loose and would have hidden them. They were tiny wheels, with the initials 'E.P.' at their centre.

Lishe Parsons clearly believed that *all* of his stock should carry his mark.

Emmie-Lou had kept her word. Not only had she said nothing at all while they were still within the confines of Fort Gilman, but she had said nothing since. Twice Herne had asked her if she wanted a mouthful of water from one of the canteens, and each time she had simply nodded mutely, and taken it from him without a word of thanks.

In some ways he was grateful, not having to resist her attempts to persuade him to release her, but in some ways he was disappointed. There were things about the girl that he liked, setting aside her obvious desirability. From what he'd seen of her husband, she was one of life's losers. There was nothing even remotely likeable about Elisha Parsons.

In all his days as a bounty-hunter, Jed had never once thought of himself as a hired killer. In most every town along the border there were men who would kill. Kill anyone you cared to point the finger at for as little as ten dollars. But

Jed was only for hire for legal purposes. Bring in a wanted man, or hunt a robber. Now he was bringing back a stolen girl. To him it was a job like any other. Only a little different from trying to return a rustled herd.

But it *was* a little different.

'Contract's a contract,' he said to remind himself, hardly aware he had spoken his thoughts out loud.

'What?'

'Nothing.'

'You spoke. I heard you.'

'Just thinking to myself.'

'Oh.'

'Want another drink? Plenty left. I guess we'll break for an hour in a half hour. Rest up us and the horses. Then move along to reach your spread well before sundown.'

She shook her head. 'I'm fine. I wouldn't want you worrying about me, Mister Herne.'

'If it wasn't for that sun, Mrs. Parsons, those words would have froze me clean to death.'

She didn't laugh. Didn't even smile. 'When are we going to stop? I'm tired. Didn't get that much sleep last night. Nor some of the nights before.'

'Soon be back in your own bed. Nothing like that, is there?'

She pulled up at the reins, staring him straight in the face. 'If I told you what it was like being in my own bed, with my own husband, then I doubt you'd believe it.'

There wasn't an answer to that, so Jed simply heeled his stallion on ahead, seeing a jagged set of hills, like gapped teeth, about a mile ahead, trailing away towards the south and the Mexican border, where they grew into towering peaks, eventually spilling over into the Rio Grande.

'Break there. Pass goes around it to the north, but I been this way before. There's an easy way through.'

'No Mescalero war parties?'

'One Eye wasn't leadin' what you'd have called a war party back in the old days. Last twenty years or so, and things have changed with the Indians. I know it's only six years since Yellow Hair George got himself chopped into minced meat up at the Little Big Horn, but the fighting's over. The great days when some of the plains tribes could put a couple of thousand men into the field and not notice the loss. Gone for ever.'

'Not so as I noticed, Mister Herne.'

'I'm not sayin' that what happened to you was a church picnic. But back when, things was different. Some tribes had plenty of white women. Nobody'll ever know how many. Some wagon trains just disappeared round Arizona. Men butchered, and the women and kids taken. Five years from now, and folks comin' this way'll hardly credit what happened to you.'

'Not a thing I'll ever forget.'

'No. No, I guess you won't.'

The foothills offered some protection from the sweltering heat, and Herne was glad to lead the horses to a patch of shade in a steep valley. If there had been any problems with the local Indians, he would have ridden a hundred miles to avoid going through such an obvious place for an ambush. But all was quiet to the east.

The only problem there was the occasional raid across the border by Mexican bandits, after the easy pickings of the Texas and New Mexico ranges. Fat cattle to be cut out and driven back into their own country. Sometimes the Rangers would catch a few, but most times they got away free.

It had been a great relief to the whole area when reports came back that the most ferocious of the raiders, El Capitan, had been killed by the local federales a few weeks earlier.

Herne came and lay down in the shade, leaving the horses tethered. Mrs. Parsons had unbuttoned the blouse as far as decency would allow. Maybe even a couple of buttons further, and was lying stretched out, resting her head against a smooth boulder, in one of the few clumps of grass. Eyes closed.

'How you feelin', Mrs. Parsons? Not far to go now.'

'I know that, Jed. And I'm feeling just about like you'd feel in my place.'

'I'm sorry.'

'You're *not*!'

'I *am* sorry. Doesn't change a thing. I'll still go on acting the way I did before, but I truly am sorry for you.'

Emmie-Lou sat up, rubbing a finger across the front of her skirt, hitching it up a little to show something of her leg above the top of the riding boot.

'Jed?'

'What is it?'

'You're a very handsome man.'

'And you're a damned pretty woman, but that don't and won't alter a thing.'

'I'm not saying it will. Your wife must have been very lucky.'

'I told you 'bout her on the way in from West Wind Canyon. All I'm tellin'. We met and we married and now she's a year under the ground.'

'Now it's my turn to say that I'm sorry. Guess that I'm so filled up with pity for myself that I forget that there's other folks have a bad time too.'

For a time they lay in silence. Herne closed in with dark thoughts of his past. The woman locked into nightmares about her future.

Suddenly, breaking the silence of the pass, Emmie-Lou sat up decisively. 'Jed Herne. I want you to lie with me.'

'Won't make . . .'

'I know that.'

She stood up and moved to kneel by his side, resting a

hand on his shoulder as gentle as the wing of a butterfly. He was moved by her youth, and on an impulse he laid his hand on top of hers, covering it. Squeezing it softly.

'Jed.'

'Mrs. Parsons. I figure we ought to be movin' on. Less somethin' happens we both regret.'

'Both of us?'

He sat up, so that their faces were close together. He could smell the clean scent of soap on her skin, and saw the softness of her cheeks. The eyes, so young, and so like the eyes of Louise. His heart gave a great leap with the pain of remembering and the loneliness that sat at his shoulder on the trail that wound endlessly to its inevitable end.

'Jed.'

'Emmie-Lou. You have to believe me. I . . . God knows but I'd . . . I'd like to. How the . . .? How can I when I'm goin' to take you back in a few hours? I've got to do that, and you have to . . .'

'I do understand, Jed, my dearest. I *do*. And I know what will happen. We'll never ever meet again, so . . .'

He looked deep in her eyes, and reached up, stroking her cheek with the tips of his fingers, brushing back a strand of fine hair from her forehead. Let his hand slip around the back of her neck, slowly tugging her forwards, closer to him.

Closer.

Her lips were dry, the skin cracked from the heat of the sun, tasting of salt. Hesitantly, like a deer coming to a pool, Herne touched his tongue to her lips, feeling them part, and her teeth nibble at him. Sucking him into the moist cavern of her mouth, while her arms went round him, tugging him still nearer to her.

Emmie-Lou rolled back, making Jed follow her, keeping their mouths locked together, her fingers gripping him by the shoulders, digging through his shirt to gouge at his back.

'Oh, yes,' she moaned, her eyes closed.

He kissed her again, letting his right hand inch towards the open neck of the blouse, sliding inside. Tracing through the trickle of sweat between the breasts, and cupping her body. Feeling the nipple spring up against his fingers like a tiny animal. She pushed him over to his side so that she could free one hand, touching him through the thick material of his trousers, panting through clenched teeth.

'Please, Jed. Do it.'

Instinctively he looked all around them, checking the trail ahead and back. Ranging over the tops of the ravine, making sure the horses were well tethered. Taking the Colt from the holster, and laying it on the ground near to his hand. Only then did he walk cautiously across again to where Emmie-Lou lay, legs stretched apart, a look on her face of soft arousal. She had unbuttoned the blouse to the waist, and he saw that she wore nothing beneath.

The breasts were jutting and firm, tipped with fire amid the pools of shadow. She smiled up at him as he hopped around pulling off his boots, rolling his trousers down over his ankles.

'My, my. A real gentleman. Taking off your boots first. Don't forget the hat as well, Mister Herne.'

He grinned at her, tossing the stetson on the ground with the trousers and boots, making sure again that the gun was ready to his hand.

'None of your damned insolence, Mrs. Parsons.'

'Or what'll happen to me, sir? I hope you aren't going to hurt me with that dreadful great weapon I see you have.'

It was the first time that he'd seen her behave with anything like a natural happiness, as if she was determined on a final fling before returning to the darkness of her marriage. For Jed it was a change to feel relaxed and roused with a woman. Since the death of Louise there had been so little time.

So much killing.

He knelt for a moment beside her, looking down at her, thinking how young and vulnerable she was. At that moment he was a hair's breadth from selling out the contract and riding to pay Parsons back the money he'd been paid.

Then he thought about living with himself for the next God knows how many years if he did. Just for a few minutes of lust and a girl with a baby face who'd picked the wrong man to marry. His own peace of mind wasn't worth it.

'Please, darling Jed.'

She smiled up at him, and he lay by her, kissing her tenderly on the lips, while his right hand delved under the long skirt, fondling her leg. Sliding higher, between her smooth thighs, until he reached his destination. Emmie-Lou was wearing a pair of thin cotton drawers, with ribbons tying the legs.

It only took a moment to untie them and push his hand up and through. Touching her, and finding her warm and ready for him. As his fingers made contact, she moaned and writhed, thrusting her hips hard against him, closing her legs on his wrist with surprising strength, grinding them together.

'Oh. That feels so good, Jed.'

She touched him, her hand cool on his hot swollen flesh, squeezing him and rubbing her fingers around him. He closed his eyes, trying to contain his passion.

'Jed?'

He probed at her, using his fingers to bring her to fever-pitch, and he kissed her on the mouth, feeling her gasping and moving uncontrollably under him.

'What?'

'Can't we . . .?'

'We can't do anything after this but ride on a few more hours. You want to stop this, Emmie-Lou, then I'll be damned sorry, but I'll understand. I want you.'

'I'll give you everything you want.'

'Hell. I've been offered a whole lot of things in my time. But never everything.'

'All right, Jed. I won't ask you again. I guess there isn't any point.'

'There isn't. Once you sell out, then you keep on that way. I haven't got as old as I have to finish up like that. Sorry, Emmie-Lou.'

'Then love me a little, Jed. I never got much lovin', and once Lishe gets me back there, then I guess I'm not ever goin' to get much.'

'Maybe it won't be that bad,' said Herne, knowing men well enough to be sure that what she said about her husband was dead to rights.

'So at least take me back home with the taste of a real man on my lips, and the feel of some real loving deep inside me. Love me up a damned storm, Jed Herne. So that I'll remember it for ever and a day.'

She was smiling at him as he lay close, but her eyes glistened with tears. He touched his lips to her face, tasting the wetness and the bitterness of her sadness. Then the closeness of her body roused him, and he thrust his knee between her thighs, and entered her, feeling her jerk as though she'd been struck.

'My God, yes! Oh, yes. Yes.'

The first time was too quick, both of them clawing their way to a frantic climax. As he lay on top of her, taking most of his weight on elbows and knees, the sand warm to the touch, Herne felt himself stirring again.

'Already? I didn't know that a man could ... not so soon after.'

He didn't answer, concentrating all his attentions on keeping what he'd won. It had been so long that he wasn't sure that he could. And the thought that maybe he couldn't crowded out his confidence. Emmie-Lou began to move against him, straining up her mouth to kiss him, her tongue probing in between his teeth, keeping him roused.

He felt the fluttering tightness of her stomach muscles as she readied herself for the last surge of passion, and he managed to join her, both of them collapsing panting and exhausted among the shaded boulders.

'Jed?'

'What?'

'I . . . no, it don't matter.'

'What?'

'Just that . . .' she leaned across and kissed him, very gently, on the lips. 'Just that I wanted to thank you. For what you done back in the Canyon. And for what you just done. I'll truly never forget you.'

He kissed her on the cheek, getting stiffly to his feet, brushing red sand from knees and hands. Reaching for his clothes and gun. Looking round from habit at the skyline, and finding it reassuringly clear.

'Emmie-Lou. I want you to know that I am truly sorry for all this . . .'

She stood up, as pink and naked as a peeled shrimp, and hugged him, her body pressed hard against his. 'Jed Herne, you are one Hell of a man.'

'I'll not forget you, either.' And, after a decent pause for the emotion of the moment. 'I'll never forget you, Emmie-Lou. Not ever.'

Which was a lie.

Before he met and married Louise, Jedediah Herne could not have counted either the men he'd killed or the girls he'd laid. Occasionally a face would stand out, but they were just blurs on a long, long trail. Bar-girls and faro-dealers in saloons from California to the eastern sea-board. Faces to smile at and bodies to be satisfied. And dollars to be handed over for the privilege.

Maybe he'd remember Emmie-Lou Parsons for a while. Maybe.

The rest of the ride back to Lishe's spread was as calm and peaceful and uneventful as Herne had hoped it would be. The sun scorched them from a sky as clear as the sea off Big Sur, with only a hint of a wind to keep life tolerable. Herne rubbed at his chin where traces of stubble were appearing. There hadn't been much time for shaving that morning at Fort Gilman.

'I guess 'bout another two miles. Maybe three. Should be seeing your husband's riders soon.'

'They don't come out this way often. It's poor land, and that ridge yonder cuts it off from the grazing pastures to the east.'

Since their rest during the hottest part of the day, their relationship had changed. Despite all her loving words, Emmie-Lou had grown more bitter as they neared her home, returning to the theme of begging and asking and threatening and weeping. Just for him to give her a chance.

'After what I done for you, Jed.'

'You lay back and took your pleasure of me, Mrs. Parsons, and I was grateful then. I'm still grateful. And the answer is still the same.'

'No?'

'No.'

The ridge she mentioned was a jagged spur of rock writhing out from the main body of the southern foot-hills, spreading in a barren tangle towards the Mexican border. There was no clear way through it, but a trail bent easily across the top, winding among the boulders like a brokeback rattler.

From the top it was possible to look clear over the last couple of miles to the Parsons' spread, set like a black mausoleum in the centre of a red featureless cemetery.

Neither of them spoke over the last mile to the top of the ridge. Emmie-Lou prayed for some kind of miracle. Jed tried to figure out the best way of sending the two and a half thousand dollars to where it might do most good. The greater part of it to England and the rest to buy him a better horse.

It hadn't been an easy mission, but when you got to be the best around, then not many of them were. Another fifteen minutes and it would be all over.

'There it is, Mrs. Parsons. Home again.'

The house squatted silently, like a great black toad on a strip of orange silk, and Emmie-Lou shuddered at the sight. Reined in and sat there for a moment, breathing deeply. Trying to capture the moment and hold it. Stretch it out for ever.

'Best move on.'

'Yes.'

From where they sat, they could see the land to the east, with the spine of rock straggling away to their right, northwards. And the semi-desert behind them that they had ridden, the further range of hills shimmering in the ferocious heat. Only to their right was the view obstructed. By the mountains that folded on and on towards Mexico.

Herne set his spurs to the horse, walking it forwards, when he heard the click. A sound that froze him in the saddle, wondering how many? Where? And who?

'Hold it very still, senor, or we will pick you from that horse like a flea from a whore's belly.'

Slowly he turned round, and there they were. At least a dozen. Maybe more. Mexican bandits, most wearing sombreros, except for the fat one with the Winchester aimed at Herne's guts, barely ten yards away. He had on a battered naval officer's uniform cap, its peak decorated with strips of peeling gold braid.

'El Capitan?' asked Herne, though the question wasn't really necessary.

'Si.'

'I heard you were dead.'

The Mexican laughed, showing a mixture of rotting teeth and gold fillings. 'Not me, Senor. But, very soon, you will be. You have the word of El Capitan.'

And he thumbed back the hammer of the Winchester.

Chapter Ten

They rode fast, making it hard for Herne to stay in the saddle with his wrists tried behind him. But the trail was good, with no loose stones to make a horse slip. The bandits kept close, swirling at the centre of a dust-cloud that billowed about them as they headed south. Towards the Rio Grande.

The Parsons' spread was far behind them, and Jed guessed that they'd aim to cross the border by sun-down, safe away from any American pursuit. They were within three or four miles of the Mexican line when El Capitan held up a hand and they all reined in.

Although his knowledge of Spanish wasn't that good, Jed knew enough to be able to understand what was going on. Rather than cross and get caught by darkness, they decided to go to a hide-out a mile along the river valley, up a box canyon.

El Capitan saw that Herne was listening to their conversation and heeled his horse across alongside him. 'You speak our language, amigo?'

'A little. You're camping near here?'

'Si.'

'Then back to Mexico in the morning?'

The chief laughed, and Herne recoiled from the dreadful stench of rotting teeth that gushed from his mouth.

'You hear that, my friends! This gringo thinks we go back to Mexico tomorrow.' Looking at Herne closely. 'We look maybe stupid?' Jed shook his head. 'No. Then why we want to get killed?'

'Bit of trouble with the soldiers?'

El Capitan grinned. 'You say that again. Something about a bank and a military payroll. Is the right word "Payroll"? Good. A few men fall off horses and bullets hit them. So they say that El Capitan is dead, but you see he is not. But he will not go home for a few months. Stay here and make gold from Yankees. Is good idea?'

'Is not bad idea, but what about us?'

The bandit slapped him so hard on the back that Herne nearly toppled from the saddle. But he had a shrewd idea that once he fell he might not get up again, so he fought to maintain his balance.

'We have had no time to talk, gringo. Not you or the beautiful senorita here.'

'I am a senora,' said Emmie-Lou, sitting her mare just behind Herne. 'And when my husband hears about what you have . . .'

'No,' said Herne, desperately.

Still smiling, El Capitan reached across and slapped him on the face, his leather glove cutting Jed's lip.

'You keep not talking, eh? I hear the lady. So young and lovely and married. And her husband will make us sorry. Who is your husband, lady?'

She looked at Jed, who sat very still, knowing the eyes of the bandits were on him, not daring to make any kind of move to warn her not to tell them. Plenty of times bands of killers like this might take prisoners. Sometimes they killed them straight off. Sometimes, if they were important enough, they would keep them for ransom. Most times they would let them go. Jed had guessed that the main reason they had been stopped was for the woman. And if it hadn't been for the closeness of the ranch they would have gunned him down. Having let him live this long he reckoned there was a better than average chance. Just as long as he didn't cross them up. Bandits like these were as dangerous as explosive, needing only one small spark to set them off into disastrous action.

'I ask you again, lady. Who is your man that you think he can hurt us?'

'His name is . . . is Elisha Parsons.'

'I see. Compadres, this is the Senora Parsons. Many is the time we have enjoyed the hospitality of Senor Parsons. Though his heart is light, his arm is heavy.'

'Juan by the house last summer.'

'Jesus in the open near the new wire fence.'

'Maria Garcia in the arroyo.'

'And Manuel down by the Mission of San Miguel.'

As his men spoke, El Capitan ticked them off on his stubby fingers, the golden rings glistening in the dying beams of the sun.

'That is four. Four of my friends, all killed by the good Senor Parsons in the last year.'

'But you're thieves. Rustlers. Bandits.'

'Si. All of those. And now you can add that we are also become . . . what is the word for a stealer of people?'

Herne spoke. 'Kidnappers. That's what you are.'

The Mexican laughed. 'I like you. You know that, gringo. El Capitan likes you.'

Herne grinned back. 'Then perhaps El Capitan will show his friendship by untying my hands. It is not easy to sit a horse in this way.'

'Hey, I am not that friendly, gringo. Maybe I help you with rope round your neck and the other end tied to the saddle. It help you?'

'It would, but I'll maybe stay as I am.'

'That is good. Soon we camp for a few days. And maybe we send a message to Senor Parsons about his so lovely little wife. Maybe you write it for me, gringo. If you write?'

'I write. Not good, but I write.'

El Capitan slapped him again on the shoulder. 'You and me get friends very well. Hey, and I don't know even your name, you know that. What do they call you?'

'They call me a lot of things, but my name's Jedediah Herne.'

The bandit crossed himself, and Jed heard his name repeated by the others. Suddenly the atmosphere had changed. Become more tense and unfriendly. Guns were again lifted from holsters.

'Madre de Dios! So you are the one called Herne the Hunter!'

'Yeah. You heard of me like I've heard of you?'

'We hear that some 'Paches take this Senora. Old One Eye and his amigos.'

'He was hired by my husband to bring me back. He did it on his own and killed One Eye and half of his men. If you don't let me go, then he will kill you all.'

Herne sniffed. 'Lady, you aren't helpin' one little bit.'

The Mexican translated her words to his followers, most of whom seemed only to have a smattering of English. The bandits all bellowed their laughter, and one of them called out to Herne: 'Hey, gringo! How you kill us? You bite us all to death or make a bad smell and we run away?'

El Capitan checked the laughter by holding up his Winchester, looking round at the other bandits. 'Is enough. What Senora Parsons says. Is true?'

Herne nodded. 'Is true.'

'I have heard of Herne the Hunter. Even below the Rio Grande the word has gone of a man with a fast gun who kills for money. Senor Parsons pay you well?'

'Enough.'

'How much?'

Emmie-Lou interrupted again. 'My husband thinks that I am worth two and one half thousand dollars in gold to get me back.'

'Mrs. Parsons!' said Herne in despair. 'Why the Hell don't you keep your mouth shut? The less you say the better things might be.'

The barrel of the rifle was suddenly jammed under his nose, and he looked incuriously over it into the red-rimmed eyes of the Mexican. 'Senor Herne, I would not wish to kill such a man. But you will die if you talk in such a way again.'

The sun was sinking fast over the scarred land to the west, glowing crimson, surrounded by a crown of scarlet clouds. Herne looked away from the Mexican, trying to keep calm. Knowing only too well that his life hung by the slenderest of threads. Trying to think how he could keep that thread unbroken.

'Senora. If your husband will pay that to Senor Herne the Hunter, then perhaps he will pay more to such a poor man as myself.'

'Yes. I think he would.'

Herne shook his head, but kept his mouth closed. The girl's thoughts were so clear to him that he could almost see them written large across her forehead. Like divine intervention, she reckoned that El Capitan and his men might prove to be the way out of her dilemma. As long as she wasn't actually in the house with Lishe, then there was still hope. The only thing that Jed couldn't quite understand was how she intended to stay free.

'El Capitan?'

'What is it my most lovely Senora Parsons?' The bandit

swept the crumpled hat from his greasy head and made a low bow with it.

'You may call me Emmie-Lou, if you wish.'

Light dawned on Herne. So *that* was the way she hoped to win through. Ally herself with the Mexicans against her own husband. From what he knew of El Capitan's reputation with women, he would probably go along with her plans.

For just as long as they suited him.

It wasn't any surprise for Jed to see that the girl rode the last way towards the night camp alongside the leader of the killers, their heads close together. Nor that he laughed a great deal. Nor that his hand strayed with increasing regularity to rest on her arm or across her shoulders.

For Herne the trip was painful, but he'd known worse. The Mexicans had taken the Sharps from its bucket and the Colt from the holster. But they hadn't bothered to search him properly and the bayonet was still snug inside his boot.

El Capitan must have taken lessons from the Mescalero chief. The canyon where they set up their base was wide enough at its far end for comfort, and so narrow at its opening that it was a tight squeeze for a single horseman.

The Mexicans dismounted and set about readying a meal for the night. Herne was impressed with their speed and efficiency, and he saw why El Capitan had the name he did for being a man to be feared and respected. They helped Jed from his horse and tied him to a tree at the edge of a pool almost identical with that in West Wind Canyon. His hands were roped together, and then pulled up tight to a loop around his neck. His feet were also tied with rawhide thongs, and a further cord ran around his throat, knotted tightly at the back of the tree, out of reach of his fingers. It was a good professional job and Herne didn't bother too much to test the ropes. He knew how good they were.

The girl sat by the fire with El Capitan, and every now and again she giggled, and twice laid her hand on the bandit's arm in a gesture that was as coquettish as it was simple. Herne watched it all and said nothing. There was nothing that he could say.

Food was cooked over a number of small fires, and El Capitan ordered one of his men to take some and feed their captive, and give him water to drink. The food was tacos and burritos. Hot and spicy pancakes filled with meat and vegetables. The water was welcome.

'Thank you, El Capitan,' called Herne after the man feeding him had gone. 'That is the sort of friendship that I truly value from a man like you.'

The Mexican said something to Emmie-Lou and stood up, belching loudly, waving a casual hand to acknowledge the laughter and cheers of his men. Picked up a light brown earthenware jug from near the fire and a couple of mugs and walked over to squat on his haunches alongside the bound man. Wheezing with the effort.

'I am getting too old for this game, Senor Herne. You also are young not any more.'

'Guess we're about of an age.'

'But you are so much . . . what is the word for not fat?'

'Skinny?'

El Capitan laughed. 'Skinny. Si, that is it. Why are you so much skinny than me?'

Herne laughed. 'Guess it's maybe because I done a little more runnin' than you.'

The smile vanished from the Mexican's face, replaced with a leer of animal cunning. 'You not do much running from the camp of El Capitan, do you, Senor Herne?'

'Not less'n I take this here tree with me.'

'Is good, mi amigo. Is very good. Listen, you and I must talk. We are . . . you want a little pulqué?'

Herne nodded and the bandit poured out a tumbler of the oily white liquid, holding it to his captive's lips and watching him as he drank. The fiery liquor burned at Herne's throat, but he concealed any emotion, aware of the eyes staring at him.

'Is good. Now El Capitan drinks, and then you and I will have a small talk.'

He gurgled away at the pulqué, letting it run over his thick red lips, and dribble through the stubble of his beard. Only when he had drained it did he wipe his hand across his mouth and smile once more at Herne. It was an unsettling sort of smile. Jed Herne had known a lot of killers. Some of them – the successful ones – cold self-possessed men. But there had been others. Those who killed simply because they enjoyed it. Or because they couldn't help it. Many of the latter had smiled like El Capitan did. With a smile that could vanish from the face with the speed of a flash-flood.

'Now, we talk. Men like you and me, Senor Herne, are as rare as water in the desert. Is not true?'

'Is true.'

'You been paid by old Parsons, that stinkin' son of a bitch rotten bastard! To get the woman back.'

'I've only been paid some front money. When I take her back there's more to come.'

The Mexican shook his head. 'I hear you say "when" you take her back. I think that maybe you don't mean that no more. What do you think?'

'I think maybe you're right.'

'Hey, that's good, amigo!' El Capitan slapped him hard across the shoulder, knocking him sideways, the tension of the ropes nearly strangling him. 'I guess you know the truth about this Senora?'

'Yeah. She hates her old man. But I got a contract out on her, so I aim . . . aimed . . . to take her home.'

'I tell you what I do, Herne. I goin' to get lots of dollars from that short-fisted bastard.'

'Tight-fisted bastard.'

'What?'

'Tight-fisted. That's the word. Not short-fisted. But I know what you mean.'

'Fine. Hey! Diego! Bring us some more pulqué, and make the lady have plenty drink too.' He winked at Herne. 'I think that maybe that lady, she can be . . . you know.'

His gesture with the index finger of the right hand and the palm of the left hand made it very clear what he meant. The wink and the nudge were hardly necessary.

'Maybe her husband won't like it if the merchandise gets damaged.'

'Maybe, Senor Herne. But I not damage her too much. Just a little here and there. But most of all a little there!' Again, the gesture was very explicit.

One of the Mexicans came reeling across, his thin shadow stretched out by the flickering light of the fires. Beyond him, Herne was able to see that Mrs. Parsons was being given pulqué, and was not resisting it in any way, giggling at the bandits, sitting sprawled back against one of the trees, her skirt already riding high over her boots, showing a stretch of pale skin well above the knee, and he wondered what the rest of the night would bring for Emmie-Lou.

'I tell you what I do, Senor Herne, and you tell me if I think you have a good plan.' He looked puzzled for a moment. 'I think that's not what I mean. I think I mean . . .'

Herne grinned, feeling the heat of the pulqué driving through him. He hoped that the Mexican wouldn't give him any more of the lethal liquor.

'I know what you mean, El Capitan. You mean that you have a lot of fun tonight. Tomorrow Lishe Parsons gets a message that his young wife has met with an accident and won't be there until he pays up. Am I right?'

The bandit smiled at him, his head lop-sided on his squat shoulders. 'Too right, mi compadre. Mi wonderful amigo, Senor Herne. And he pay us and she go home to his ...' he let his wrist dangle in a gesture of impotence. 'To that, amigo. A shame for such a woman. But there is no fairness in life. Is not true? Eh, is not very, very true?'

'Nothing's fair,' said Herne. 'Like a friend of mine used to reckon. Why should the churches be wide open and empty, when the prisons are locked up tight and full of folks?'

El Capitan looked at him in bewilderment for a moment, until the truth seeped through the fumes of pulqué. Then he began to laugh and laugh.

He was still laughing when he stood up and walked back to the fire. Where Emmie-Lou waited giggling for him.

Chapter Eleven

They put on shows like that at some of the more expensive cat-houses in plenty of cities all the way from Washington to Tijuana. Jed Herne had always been a player of that sort of game rather than a spectator, but right now he didn't have a lot of choice.

He figured that it had been Emmie-Lou taking a little petty revenge on him for his honouring the contract. She was the one who led the way to the patch of ground, away from the main group of bandits, directly in front of Herne, pulling El Capitan along by the hand. Guiding him, though he was so drunk that he could hardly walk. Emmie-Lou was much the worse for alcohol, and she kept tripping over tree roots, and sniggering to herself.

Pausing to bend over the bound Herne and tweak him hard on the cheek. 'Now you really see something, old man. Maybe show you what you given up on. Least this Mex knows what he's goin' to get.'

'You sure about what you're doin'?'

'Mister Herne wants to know if I know what I ... if I think I know what I'm doing.'

El Capitan paused in the act of tugging off his white cotton trousers to stagger about laughing. 'I know what I am up to, and you know soon what will be up you.'

Herne glanced across the clearing at the Mexican's body, and he grinned ruefully. 'Don't know about anything else, Mrs. Parsons, but he's taken so much pulqué on board that I doubt he could even raise an anchor, never mind nothin' else.'

She looked round, and then bent down to kneel by him, and he saw the veil of alcohol lift for a moment, revealing the frightened girl beneath.

'You're so damned upright and proper, aren't you, Herne? Well he might not be up to much in terms of what the wives of Magdalena might find right and acceptable. But he's going to be the way that I ride on free away from Lishe.'

'He tell you that?'

'Surely did. He's going to get the money from miserable old Lishe, and then he says I can go. In return I let him do what he wants.'

Jed closed his eyes. 'You go right ahead, Emmie-Lou. I know there's not a thing I can do or say that'll change your mind, and I'm not even goin' to try.'

'You're just jealous of me.'

'Come on, pretty Senora. El Capitan does not like to be kept waiting.'

'Coming.' To Herne: 'I want you to watch and see what happens and eat your heart out. Think that it could be you. Not just for one night but for a whole lot more.'

Glancing across her shoulder at the waiting Mexican she deliberately touched Jed, stroking his body and pursing her lips as if she was going to kiss him. Instead she spat at him, and laughed.

'There. Not so big and powerful now, are you, Jedediah? Still taking me back?'

'Hurry up my little eagle. Part of me is losing cold for you.'

Emmie-Lou tugged open her blouse so that Jed could see the peaked cones of her breasts, fire-tipped in the red glow. She watched his eyes, still touching him with her left hand, low down in the shadows where the Mexicans couldn't see. Grinning at him as she felt his response. Deliberately poking out her tongue and running its red tip across the gleaming white teeth.

'You'd just love to be him, wouldn't you? To be lying on the ground between my legs? Ramming that up inside me like a stallion with a brood mare?'

There was no point in denying it, as his body betrayed the lie, so Herne said nothing. Which infuriated the girl more than words would have.

'Well you won't have the pleasure! Not ever!'

She stood up, legs astride, glaring down at him. Then deliberately raised her foot in the heavy riding boot and brought it down on his groin, grinding the heel into his erect manhood.

Jed passed out, unaware that he had screamed, high and thin like a steer at the gelding. When he came round he was still bound, and his shirt and trousers were covered in his own vomit. The pain in his genitals was agonizing, but bearable. He'd known worse, and there was the consolation that it could only get better from now on.

He doubted that she'd done him any permanent damage, except maybe to his pride. The trousers were thick enough to protect him from the worst of the kick.

Emmie-Lou and El Capitan were oblivious to him, locked together in a tangle of pale flesh, barely visible in the darkness of the canyon. Herne could hear them both moaning, and once Emmie-Lou cried out with what sounded like a mixture of shock and pain and desire. Despite the pulqué, the bandit seemed able to perform sufficiently well for the drunken woman to derive enjoyment. Tied as he was Herne could neither lie down nor comfortably turn his head to look elsewhere.

He quite deliberately allowed himself to slip away from the present, letting his mind roam back to the good thoughts of the past. And his dead wife. The men who'd been responsible and the manner of each of their deaths. Almost without his realizing it, sleep came unbidden to Herne the Hunter.

He woke three or four times during the night, disturbed by a movement among the rocks, or by a log shifting and breaking on one of the fires. He wasn't sure when the girl and El Capitan left, but the space where they had been was empty well before the moon showed midnight.

The Mexicans were careful, even in such a secure hideout, keeping at least two sentries alert and on the move throughout the night. The tightness of the ropes meant that Herne's muscles locked with cramp, and it was hard to try and get enough freedom of movement to ease the pain.

Dawn brought some relief.

The naval cap perched on the back of his head, El Capitan came lurching from among the trees, rubbing his face and belching.

'That is too much, my gringo compadre. When a man gets to our age, then it is time to say adios to women or to drink. Both together are bad.'

'How's Emmie-Lou?'

'Being very sick. She falls sleeping while I am still ready

for making love to her. So I show her a new way, and she wake up quick.'

He laughed, then groaned and held his forehead. 'I should not be so laughing, Senor Herne. Also that is not good for me.'

'I'll bet it wasn't great for her, either,' said Jed, grimacing as pain from his cramped legs hit him.

'You hurt?'

'Some.'

'Wait. José! Come and untie Senor Herne. But bring Alfredo and both keep guns on him. I think he is man who might bring trouble to us.'

'Not right now,' said Jed, watching the two bandits approaching him with knives drawn. El Capitan had Herne's own Colt in his hand, the hammer drawn back. His stubby finger ready on the narrow trigger.

'Do not stand before my gun, José, or the hole I shoot might be in your belly. His feet leave tied, but loose. So he walk but not run. That's good. And his left hand. Behind his back and to his neck. Is very good. Now you come and sit and you eat and write a letter for me. I talk American pretty damned good. No?'

'Yes. Very well.'

'But I not write so good.' The barrel of the revolver gaped at Herne's skull. 'I think good to see what you write and know if you try a trick.'

'You tell me what you want, and by God, you'll get it. I'm not going to get my head blown apart for that stupid little girl.'

'That's good. Mucho good! We and I are men of the same . . . what is word for men like us?'

'Killers?'

'Hey, that's a . . . No. Is no good. I mean we are like brothers.'

'Same sort of breed?'

'Si. Like stallions. We are same age and we both live by gun. We not fight over woman. Come here with me, gringo, and I help you walk to fire and food.'

With the arm of the Mexican supporting him, Herne was able to stagger the few steps to sit heavily by the smouldering remains of one of the night's fires. There was a heavy metal pan of greasy stew simmering and El Capitan helped him to a bowl, filled to the brim. And a silver spoon, beautifully ornamented. Jed looked at it, and held it up in the air, showing it to the bandit.

'Si. Is very lovely. We get a hundred like it from a big church not far from San Simeon di Compostella. A fat church with fat priests. I ask you, Senor Herne, is it right that such stinkin' pigs have a hundred of such spoons of silver while we are hungry. Our bellies flap at our backs. So I take the spoons, and they cry out.'

'I'll bet.'

'So loud that I stop my ears, but still I hear them like old women whose blankets have been taken.'

'So?'

'So, Senor Herne, I think that maybe they are so unhappy that they do not want to live with no spoons.'

'And?' asked Jed, guessing the answer.

'So I give them what they want and I shoot them all. No more sad priests with no spoons.'

The Mexican looked miserably at Herne eating the stew, awkwardly balancing the bowl on his knee.

'And I tell you another thing. They get damned dirty too quick those spoons.'

Emmie-Lou didn't appear for the best part of an hour, and when she did she looked ten years older. Her eyes were swollen from crying and her skin was sallow, almost green. She walked across and helped herself to a mug of coffee, ignoring both Herne and the Mexicans. El Capitan took no notice of her, carrying on telling Herne a story about the time that he and some of his compadres robbed a village near the border.

'I was not the man I am now, you see. But our chief then was a great man. Calvera. We always took food from this stinkin' hole and one year we leave them a small piece more. So they use the money and buy guns. How many I do not know but I think maybe seven. Americanos. Killers. We had no chance.'

'I heard something of that,' said Jed, wondering when he might get a chance to use the heavy knife in his boot.

'They kill many of us. And Calvera. A saint, Senor Herne. Who would give the shirt from his back to help a poor man. So many killed.'

'Heard the village stayed safe after that.'

El Capitan laughed again, throwing back his head and spilling black coffee on the dry soil. 'You hear not so good. We leave them two years. Then I and some other amigos visit that place again.'

'And?'

'This time we do not leave them too much. Madre de Dios, but we help them! Each man we give two paces of land. Each house that is old we burn so they can make again. Each woman and girl we give honour of knowing us. All of us. Many times. That place will not again buy guns from north of Rio Grande.'

Some of the other bandits had been sitting around and they all clapped and shouted at the words of their leader. Herne wondered if it was true. He'd known most of the men who'd gone south to swat away some flies. Nearly gone himself. Chris, and Lee. Vinny. The others. No, El Capitan wouldn't make it up. It had to be true.

Still laughing, the chief rose and walked away, leaving three of his men leaning on their rifles to watch Herne and the girl. She still kneeled across the fire from him. He looked at her, and saw that her blouse was torn. Her skirt ripped all the way up one side. Her boots were missing and the soles of her feet were covered in red sand. On her neck there were the marks of burns, and from where he was sitting, Jed could see the livid bruises inside her thighs.

'How you feeling, Mrs. Parsons?' he asked her quietly.

Her voice was cold as death. Empty of emotion. Flat and wasted. 'I'm sorry for what I did to you, last night. I was drunk. I shall never drink again.'

'What about El Capitan? He going to be your knight on a white horse?'

'Don't Jed. I've had enough.' She lowered her head and he saw that she was crying. The golden ear-rings tinkled softly, almost buried in the mane of tangled hair that hung over her shoulders.

'There's not a way out. You know that. He gets the money and he kills you. No reason not to. He takes you back to Lishe and maybe he gets killed. No. He'll take the gold and run right back across the big river.'

'I guess that's right. But maybe even dying's better than going home.'

'Maybe it is. For you. Not for me, Mrs. Parsons. I'm a man who wants to live. No matter what. Give up on the idea of living and next thing you know the lid's being screwed down on top of you.'

'What can I do?'

'Wait and watch. Maybe there'll be a break for us.'

'If we get away from them . . . Will you still . . .?'

'Surely. Don't make no difference to me. Indians or greasy Mex bastards. Just like Hell and high water. If I'm still breathin', then I'll take you back. One way or another.'

The council of the bandits lasted until near mid-day, when they came back and sat around their two captives. El Capitan held out his hand and one of the other Mexicans gave him a piece of paper and a chewed stub of pencil.

'Here. You write we have her, and that we want ten thousand dollars American to let her go.'

'You want me to spread that out a mite?'

'What is "spread out", Senor Herne?'

'You just want that, like you said? Or maybe with a few bits of extra? Like a coat of paint or two?'

'No. Like I say it. And put it is from you. That way he believe it.'

Jed nodded and took the pencil, smoothing the paper over his knee, and finding he couldn't cope with the breeze with his left hand tied. He looked at El Capitan, who shook his head.

'No, amigo. Not that much for Herne the Hunter. Maybe with one leap you will be free of us. The Senora hold the paper and you write. Then you read it to me. Then I look at it to see no trick.'

Emmie-Lou kneeled down silently, keeping the paper from fluttering away, while Jed laboriously wrote out the letter, his tongue between his teeth with the effort of spelling. While the couple of dozen Mexicans watched him, he scribbed away, sweating with the effort.

'There.'

'Read.'

'Mister Parsons. I regret to inform you that I have got your wife from the Apaches, only for us both to fall into the hands of some Mexicans, and their chief El Capitan and they are holding your wife for money. They want ten thousand dollars in American money. I am sorry but I cannot do anything to aid. Your humble and obedient servant, Jedediah Travis Herne.'

'Is good. Is very good. I send Manuel and Alfredo to the house with it. They back here by night. With money, then you can go free.'

'Both of us?'

The Mexican beckoned Herne to stand and follow him a

few paces away from the rest. Hobbled as he was, Jed found it hard to walk, but he managed it, ignoring a desperate look from the woman. El Capitan laid a hand on his shoulder and breathed fumes of bad teeth and spiced food in his face.

'We are men of the word. Is right way?'

'Men of the world.'

'Si. World. How can I let her free? To do that will put guns after me and my men. She will bring the Rangers to us. Maybe the federales also.'

'I'll take her. Instead of you and your men. Let me add to the letter saying that. Then, you get the gold, and then I ride along to the spread with her.'

'That way you live also, Senor Herne. Maybe get your gold also from Senor Parsons.'

At the mention of the name of Lishe, El Capitan spat noisily in the sand. Herne grinned. 'Might at that. That way I live and you live and the girl lives. Seems to me that's the only way we all get what we want.'

The Mexican walked a few paces away, stroking the side of his face with one hand. Keeping his eyes turned away from Jed. Speaking to the grove of trees, and the red canyon walls beyond.

'Is good idea you have, and I think that maybe I do that. I do not want to hurt Senora Parsons, but I do not like her man. Him I would hurt if I can. So maybe we do what you say. Now I send Alfredo and Manuel to get money. You put the bit more and that make him sure we do not try any trick on him? Yes?'

'Yes,' said Herne, feeling that he would trust an angry rattler further than he'd trust El Capitan.

It had been six hours since the two bandits had ridden away. The guard on the mouth of the ravine suddenly waved a hand over his head. All of the others stood and watched for the signal. One hand open. Then a closed fist. Nothing more.

El Capitan turned to Emmie-Lou, his face slick with anger.

'You better start to pray, Senora. He say that one man rides back here. And a dead man with him. You better pray one damned lot.'

It was Alfredo hanging dead over the saddle of his horse, led in by Manuel. Alfredo had been flogged to death. With a snakeskin whip that had taken the skin off his body in long curling strips. Off his back. Stomach. Chest. Face.

Manuel had not been beaten.

But Parsons had personally taken a butcher's knife, and while his men held the screaming man still, he had hacked all of the fingers off his left hand.

'He say he leave me a hand to ride with. And he leave me tongue to speak his words.'

The Mexican chief stood calm and still, and Herne felt a pang of cold fear, sensing that the wings of death fluttered low over him.

'What were those words, mi compadre, that he did not hear what our good Americano, Senor Herne the Hunter put for us?'

He turned to look at Jed, and his eyes were flat and expressionless as shaded pools. Black and still like the eyes of a dead snake.

'He say he do not believe we have his woman, and that Senor Herne lies to him.'

El Capitan nodded. 'I see that. He wishes to have . . . what is word, mi amigo?'

Herne looked at him. 'He wants proof.'

'Si. Senor Parsons wants proof. Then we will give him some proof. Senora Parsons, come here.'

As she walked slowly towards him, like someone locked in a nightmare, the Mexican reached at his belt and drew out a long knife.

Chapter Twelve

Emmie-Lou bled a lot when they cut off her right ear.

Herne watched with a dispassionate interest as El Capitan ordered two of his men to hold her while he performed the operation himself. She screamed and fought, kicking out with bare feet, but the men were too strong for her. The knife sliced through neatly and quickly, one of the Mexicans tying a wad of rag to the side of her head to check the bleeding. Not that she was aware of that. At the first touch of the cold steel her eyes rolled up into her skull and she passed out.

'She will not look too bad,' said El Capitan, handing the shell of pink gristle to one of his men, the distinctive golden ear-ring gleaming. 'Maybe she grow her hair to hide it. I think it not make her husband not like her. What she said last night he don't like her too much. Is right, eh gringo?'

Herne sniffed. 'I guess an ear or two either way won't make a Hell of a lot of difference to their loving man and wife union.'

'Now I send it to Senor Parsons, so that he know that El Capitan is not a man who says he has what he does not have. And this time it will be twenty thousand dollars. You tell him that, Senor Herne.'

The letter was longer, and tasked Jed's spelling even more. The chief wanted detailed plans for what was to happen and how the money was to be delivered.

'Put in that if he shoots or anything to my men who bring this letter, then I send him next the lovely eyes of his wife, and then she will not be so lovely. I am ended with playing at this napping.'

'Kidnapping, it's called.'

'Sure. Is good he knows this. He sends gold to where I say in two days time. I send all my men but maybe three or four to meet him. Make sure all is good. They come back with half gold, and then ride to meet Parsons and his vaqueros with his wife. Is good plan?'

'He'll never pay that. You're crazy to think that he will.'

Like a flash of lightning from a clear sky, El Capitan's mood changed. The point of the knife, still streaked with the pale, silvery threads of Emmie-Lou's blood, pricked at Herne's throat, and he could feel the Mexican's tension quivering through the blade.

'You ... don't ... say ... El Capitan ... is crazy! You better know that, mi amigo.'

Herne felt his mouth fill with saliva, but he didn't dare to swallow, so hard was the knife pressing at his throat. Barely moving his lips, he said: 'Kill me and no letter. No letter no plan. No plan and no gold.'

The pain eased and the Mexican sat back, first wiping the knife on Herne's shirt. 'You much like me. Not scared of any man. I like you, compadre. Like you. And when El Capitan likes a man, then he helps him. After you do letter for me, then I talk again. You like what I say.'

He rose to his feet and left Herne alone.

A half hour drifted by and Emmie-Lou Parsons came over and sat beside him. The rag was still tied to her head, making her look like a refugee from a war. Dried blood was crusted brown on the bandage, trickling down her cheek and vanishing into the neck of her blouse. She was still bare-footed.

'What's goin' to happen to me, Jed? I just seem to have reached the bottom and I can't see no way back.'

Herne had a good idea what was going to happen. El

Capitan was playing it clever. By asking so much more, but by making it clear he intended to take only half for openers, he would make Parsons ready to double-cross him. Probably ambushing him and his men when they brought back the girl, thus saving at least half the ransom and maybe all.

But Jed had a high opinion of the animal cunning of the Mexican chief. *His* thinking ran on slightly different lines. Unless Herne missed his guess, the wily bandit intended to risk the loss of most of his band, reckoning that the rancher would try treachery. El Capitan would find some excuse, with two or three of his most trusted comrades, to remain behind with the girl.

When the first half of the gold arrived, they would kill Emmie-Lou and ride away having got ten thousand dollars American for nothing. Parsons would be left with the body of his wife and probably a raging gun-battle with the remaining bandits when it was clear the girl wasn't going to be produced.

It was so crazy that it would probably work. If it meant the girl dying, then Jed would be sorry. But if it came to a choice between himself and Emmie-Lou, then he'd be ready to pull the trigger on her himself. Ultimately, there was only that one law:

Do unto others – before they do it unto you.

'Jed. Tell me.'

'What?'

'Tell me that it's all going to be fine. That Lishe'll pay and they won't kill me.'

'I'm sure as I can be that his pride'll make him want to get you back at any cost.'

He avoided any mention of the second part of the question, because he could see no way that El Capitan was going to let the girl live and finish up with her testifying against him. Whitey Coburn, Jed's old riding friend, had known the

James boys well. Jesse had often said the safest way of making sure nobody tells on you was to kill them all. And that was true whatever the crime and whoever the killers.

'How about you, Jed? You're going to miss out on all the money you earned. God knows, but you surely did enough in West Wind Canyon to get some of it.'

'From what I've seen of your husband, I don't reckon that he's the type of man to take kindly to having to pay twice for the same thing.'

'But that's not fair.'

'Lots of things in life aren't fair, Emmie-Lou. Figure you know that as well as most. But you pay your own price to live with yourself on your own terms. Lishe Parsons and I did a deal. Didn't shake hands on it, but there wasn't any need for that. Contract said I brought you back. If the Mex releases you to him, then I've not done what I promised. I'd do the same.'

She put her head on one side, as though seeing Herne for the first time. 'There's something of the Mexican in you. And something of Lishe. Some of their worst hard qualities. Ruthless and deadly. Cold, even. But you're a better man, Jed.'

He tipped his hat. 'Well, thanks a lot for that, ma'am. I guess that ain't truly what I'd call much of a compliment.'

'Senor Herne!'

'Got to go, Emmie-Lou. You take care now.'

Awkwardly, struggling to maintain his balance, Jed walked slowly over to where the bandits stood grouped around El Capitan. The injured Manuel sat on a large boulder, nursing his maimed hand inside his shirt, his face pale and sweating.

'Join, us, mi amigo. We talk of what to do, and we think that the plan we talk of is best.'

Herne nodded. 'So that's what you'll do?'

The bandit smiled, his stained teeth barely visible in the

rotting cavern of his mouth, pitched into shadow as the sun began to decline to the west of the arroyo.

'Si. Is what we will do.'

The letter was written and sent, with two more of El Capitan's lieutenants trusted with the mission. A mission that Herne himself would not have found attractive. From what he knew of Parsons, the man's pride might work two ways. One of them would insist that he retained his wife at any price. The other was that he would never deal with people like the Mexican bandits and he could easily nail them to the wall of the house and slice away a few more pounds of flesh each day.

They had left at first light, and Herne had again been tied up during the night, and just as closely guarded.

Emmie-Lou had been moved away from him, as though El Capitan no longer wanted them to talk together. The bandit chief made no attempt to interfere with her that night, totally ignoring her like a spent bullet. But Herne was included in the final planning session, as though the Mexican somehow wanted to draw him into the conspiracy.

It was going to be like Jed had suspected. El Capitan would stay behind in the canyon, with just four men, to guard the prisoners and take charge of the whole operation. He told his men that it would be dangerous if he were to risk meeting Parsons eye to eye as his hatred was so great that he might shoot down the rancher in his anger and ruin the whole deal.

And his men believed it.

As Jed lay relaxing against a tree, the bandit came grinning up to him, a jug of pulqué spilling from his chubby fingers.

'Time for another talk which is so much interesting to us, amigo.'

'I'll talk but not drink. My head's not recovered from last time.'

'The Senora Parsons. Her head is not well? Nor only her head that was hurt, eh?'

A bellow of ribald laughter that sent a couple of the horses whinnying across the branches of the corral. 'Not only her head, my old friend.' The laughter disappeared and was replaced immediately by a more serious face. 'And it is of friends that I wish to talk. Come.'

He walked away among the grove of trees, out of sight of the others, with Herne, ankles linked with rope, joining him. Once he was sure that none of the other bandits could hear them, El Capitan pulled Jed to him, his lips so close to Jed's ears that the foul miasma of his breath ruffled the hairs on the nape of his neck.

'You think my plan, she is a good one?'

'I think it is.'

'Ah. But we are men of thinking the same. So you can see my mind. What you *really* think will happen.'

Casually, as if it was doing it on its own without his agreement, El Capitan's right hand dropped to rest on the butt of his gun. Jed's Colt. And his eyes flicked at Jed's face, as if they sought the inside of his mind. It was difficult to know what to say.

'I think,' said Herne slowly, 'I would rather be on your side of the plan than on anyone else's side.'

'Good. You think like me. Maybe we long-losing brothers, eh?'

'Yes. For once I think maybe you've got it just right. Just right.'

'Now, if my plan works good, like we think. Then this will not be a good place to be, as Senor Parsons might think you have done something with this.'

'Guess he might, at that.'

'So, I like you, Herne the Hunter. And I do all right with you.'

'I'm grateful for that. Matter of fact, right now I'm damned grateful for most anything.'

'Even when we are enemies . . . is right word . . .? When we are enemies, I still help you. When my men come back here, pretty soon now, I help you one lot.'

As he strolled away, leaving Herne to struggle along after him, the Mexican was whistling to himself. Jed watched him and said, very much to himself: 'With enemies like you, then a man sure doesn't need friends.'

Chapter Thirteen

Everything had gone well. The two bandits were jubilant on their return, whooping their way through the narrow neck of the canyon, lashing their horses on to a gallop, hauling them up on their back legs while they shouted the news to the rest of the gang.

Emmie-Lou came out to watch them, turning to look to Herne in bewilderment at the calling and hooting. 'What are they saying, Jed?'

'That your husband thought about it and agreed. That they left him rolling on the floor weeping and tearing out his hair. Biting on broken teeth, they reckon. For me, I think that last bit is just for effect. But the deal's on. Twenty thousand dollars in gold. They ride and collect half of it tomorrow around mid-day. Two men bring it back here. They take you with them, and collect the rest of the gold. Easy as falling off a log.'

'He promised me ... El Capitan, that he'd just take the money and let me go. Cross up Lishe. He promised and I did all ... all of those things with him. For him. I even ...'

'I know the things you did, Emmie-Lou. Some folks are born winners. Guess you just aren't among them.'

'He promised me. Swore I could trust him. You sons of bitches are all the same.'

'Mrs. Parsons. I never promised you anything.'

As she turned away, she was crying again.

The night passed.

In the morning, soon after first light, the canyon became almost deserted as most of the band rode off to collect the gold. Herne noticed that there was a hasty meeting between El Capitan, the three men who were to remain as guards, and the two men who were to bring back the money for the first part of the exchange.

With a loud clattering of hooves on the stones, echoing around the canyon, the bandits rode off. In the sudden silence, Herne again heard the sound of the girl crying. Knowing that for the others the day was just beginning. For her it was very nearly over.

El Capitan walked to Jed, his arm round the crippled Manuel – one of the men staying behind. He said something to him, and then sent him off towards the horses. The other two guards – Jesus and Esposito – sat near Emmie-Lou. Grinning like a cat that's got the best of the cream, El Capitan came towards Herne, his naval cap perched at a rakish angle at the back of his head. Jed's gun was still in his holster. The Sharps rifle lay alongside his blanket roll. Herne had seen it there.

'Now we talk. Over here.'

The rope between his ankles had stretched a little, and Jed was able to walk more easily than before. The thongs that tied his left wrist to the back of his neck were also looser than they had been. While the other three bandits were occupied elsewhere, it might have been the chance to reach for the bayonet and attack El Capitan.

Might have been, but wasn't.

'Stand there. Soon Manuel will come and he will cut the foot ropes. Then you will get on your horse. Ride with mi compadre out of the canyon, and away. Never we meet again, if the good God is happy for that.'

'My guns?'

'No. They stay. You get more guns but never get another life, Senor Herne the clever Hunter. You ride away and never come back here. Is good?'

Jed nodded, watching Manuel lead his horse towards him, seeing Emmie-Lou rising to her feet, unable to understand what could be going on. It was at the back of his mind that it might be a cruel trap, but there was no reason for it. His usefulness to the Mexicans was over, and all they needed to do was put a bullet through the back of his head. No, El Capitan, with his odd idea of loyalty and kinship was really going to send him on his way.

'You shake hand with me, Senor?'

'Gladly.' They clasped hands, Jed feeling the palm of the bandit's hand slippery with sweat, his own dry with tension. He glanced across to Emmie-Lou. 'The girl?'

'Take what is given, amigo. If the good Lord had not wanted her to be carved, then he would not have made her such a pretty piece of meat.'

'All right.' There wasn't anything else to say. As soon as he was gone, the girl's life would be measured in minutes. And when the gold came, she was dead.

'Jed!'

'Vaya con Dios, amigo.'

'Jed! Jed Herne!!'

'So long, Emmie-Lou.'

'Please! Jed! Please.'

He didn't look back. Not once. Letting his horse walk along the narrow trail behind Manuel, ignoring her cries. Hardening his face and his soul. Not even turning to see her standing alone.

His left hand was still tied up, and he asked the bandit if he would be released.

'When out of arroyo,' replied Manuel, holding the reins awkwardly in his uninjured hand, the Colt ready at his hip in case Herne was crazy enough to try anything on his way to freedom.

The long and winding trail wound back to the open plain, hidden from outside by a great cleft in the orange rock. As soon as they were through the narrow gap, Manuel beckoned Herne alongside him, reaching in his belt for a knife, letting go of the reins.

'Here. I cut you.'

'No. I cut you,' said Herne, his right hand snaking down to draw the razor-edged bayonet from his right boot, the blade hissing from the soft leather of its sheath.

Manuel was already close to him, leaning out of the saddle with his own knife ready to cut free Jed's left hand. With his other hand fingerless, he wasn't able to pull himself away from the whistling arc of death in Herne's hand, his mouth falling open in horror and shock as he saw his own doom upon him.

The thin-bladed bayonet sliced through the side of his neck, just below the ear and a little behind it. Cutting a red-lipped gash through the swelling artery. Blood jetted out around the knife in a great crimson fountain, splattering all over Jed, his horse, and the rocks around.

'Madre . . .!'

The rest was drowned in blood welling from Manuel's mouth, choking him. His good hand went, too late, for his gun, but the lines were already going down between his brain and his body, and he slowly toppled sideways, landing with a dull thud in the dust, nearly turning a somersault as he dropped.

The blood flowed more slowly as the supply drained away into the dry earth. The eyes were still open, staring up at Herne, but Manuel saw nothing but the mistiness of death clouding the bright day into darkness.

'Adios, amigo,' said Herne, reaching round with the bloodied knife to cut his left hand free of the rope, flexing and bending the stiffness from it.

Holding the reins of his horse carefully, he bent down over the corpse and hooked the Colt from Manuel's holster. Testing the action over and over to make sure it worked. That the gun didn't play any tricks of its own that might end in his death instead of anyone else's.

Herne remounted and slowly walked the horse forwards, through the squeezed neck of the canyon, back towards the camp of the Mexicans. Stopping a couple of hundred yards from the smoking fires to tether the mount to some rocks, carrying on the rest of the way on foot. Cautiously he stepped among the tumbled boulders, eyes searching for the three remaining bandits.

Seeing two of them sitting across from the main cooking fire, smoking and talking. They had their backs to him, and beyond them he could see the woman. Jesus and Esposito both had rifles at their sides. There was no sign of El Capitan, though Herne knew that he must be somewhere around the trees at the far end of the arroyo.

He didn't have a lot of time. It would have been tactically sound to wait and grab a chance to reach one of the rifles. Then pick off all three of them when they came together in the open. But there was no way of knowing when the other pair would return with the gold.

'Has to be now,' he said to himself, trying to work out a plan that would get him close enough to the other two.

Using his own Colt he might have chanced it even at fifty or sixty paces. With Manuel's gun he needed to be a whole lot closer.

There was only one plan that suggested itself to him. The simplest of all. Just walk up to them and gun both bandits down as soon as he got close enough. Not the most cunning of strategems, but it was about the best he could come up with in the circumstances.

He moved the fingers of his right hand, and drew the gun two or three times for balance. It was clumsy compared to his own Colt, but he reckoned he could manage. No point in fretting over it. If he managed then he'd be all right. If he didn't, then he'd be dead. And everyone knew the dead had no worries.

As quietly as possible he stepped out from cover and began to walk at a steady, even pace towards the backs of Jesus and Esposito. The small pebbles and sand crunched under his boots, but the Mexicans were deep in conversation and didn't hear him coming. Not until Emmie-Lou looked up and saw him and cried out, unable to check herself.

'Quien es?' said Jesus, spinning round, and reaching for the rifle.

'Just me,' said Herne, keeping on walking, holding his arms away from his sides to show how innocent he was of any unpleasant motive. Then let them ease back down again.

'Where is Manuel?' said Esposito. Neither man was standing, unsure of the tall gringo who walked at them. Both of them had rifles, and he would not be such a crazy man when he had no gun.

'You have a gun,' said Jesus, unbelievingly, putting his hand to the ground to help himself up. Which meant he couldn't stand up and shoot at the same moment. And that turned out to be a fatal mistake for him.

By looking calm and confident, Herne had managed to cross the ground nearer to them. When Jesus started to move, and Esposito began to swing the rifle round on his knee, Jed was only thirty paces from them. Still walking.

Esposito started to shout something out, but Herne never heard what it was. He drew and fired the Colt, finding the action stiff compared to his own gun. Watched with a detached calmness as the bullet hit the sitting man in the face, ripping through his nose with a sickly cracking noise.

'High and right,' said Herne, correcting his aim and firing again.

Esposito had dropped the rifle, clutching at his face, and the second shot hit him under the right arm, smashing a rib before it ripped his lungs to bloody tatters, ending in the upper part of the heart. The bandit keeled slowly over sideways, rolling on his face in the sand. The hands still groped at his face, but he was very dead.

Jed was vaguely aware of a thin wailing, which part of his mind tabulated and decided it must be Emmie-Lou Parsons screaming. But he ignored the noise, concentrating on firing at the other Mexican, Jesus, who was rising and trying to bring up the rifle at the same time.

It took two bullets to kill him. One surprising Herne by dropping low and left, knocking the heel off the bandit's right boot, spinning him off balance.

'Hell!' spat Herne, cocking and aiming again.

The second bullet drilled through the centre of the man's chest, just a little to the left of the breast-bone, almost lifting him off his feet with the impact of the heavy slug. Jesus moaned softly as he fell backwards. A strangely muted noise, as if he had been caught by a pang of toothache.

Then he fell back, arms spread-eagled in a crucified position. Quite still, blood bubbling silently from the neat hole at the middle of his once-white shirt.

Alert for any sign of El Capitan, Herne glanced at the corpse. 'Sorry, Jesus, but I can't stick around for the third day.'

Emmie-Lou was still crying, hands to her face, great tears coursing through her fingers and dripping into the sand near her bare feet.

'Where the Hell is El Capitan?'

'He . . . Oh, my God! He went into the trees there. I think he went for a . . .'

'I don't need the details.'

From where he stood, Jed could see the Sharps rifle lying in his bed-roll. He was only forty or fifty yards from the trees, which meant that the Mexican was either hiding and waiting for Jed to come in after him.

Or . . .

'There! Climbing!'

Jed didn't need the cry from Emmie-Lou. He'd spotted the dark figure of the chief, scrabbling his way against the red rocks, already over a quarter of the way up the face, on his way to safety. Knowing the reputation of Herne the Hunter, and having probably witnessed the deaths of Jesus and Esposito, he had clearly decided that discretion was the only way of saving his life.

But he'd forgotten the rifle.

Using the long, heavy Sharps, Jed once hunted the lumbering buffalo. A gun like that could bring down one of the great beasts of the prairies at a half mile. El Capitan was a whole lot nearer than that.

Taking his time, he strolled past the two bodies towards the long gun, bending over and checking it carefully. Finding it was still loaded, as he generally carried it. Blowing dust off the stock, and rubbing with a finger at a smear of grease near the trigger.

'Hurry up. He's going.'

'Don't worry, Mrs. Parsons. The Mex isn't going anywheres at all.'

He glanced up at where the bandit was now better than halfway towards the top of the rocks. Scrambling upwards, the hat still stuck to the back of his head. A dark patch of sweat clearly visible on his shirt.

Carefully, Jed adjusted the sights, estimating the range at two hundred and fifty yards. Not an easy shot aiming at such an angle. He licked the forefinger of his right hand, setting the bead of spit on the tip of the foresight to make it stand out more clearly. Eased back on the hammer and walked towards the jagged stump of an old barren tree, forked about five feet from the ground.

'He'll be away!'

'Reckon not,' he replied, ignoring the near hysteria of the woman.

'Hurry up and kill him. Don't let him get away, Jed! Don't let him!'

'Quiet down, Mrs. Parsons. Nobody's gettin' away from me. Nobody at all.'

He settled the end of the barrel of the long gun in the notch in the tree, squinting along it. Changing the setting of the back sight a single click higher. Seeing the small figure of the Mexican, now almost within arm's reach of the top of the cliff. If he missed El Capitan, there wouldn't be a chance of a second shot.

Gentle as rousing a woman, Herne laid his finger against the cool metal of the trigger. Cuddling the polished wooden stock against the shoulder, to avoid the heavy recoil of the Sharps. Firing with both eyes open, as many top marksmen always have.

Squeezing.

Squeezing.

The crack of the shot echoed flatly around the canyon, speeding the bullet on its way. A cloud of powder obscured the man on the rock face for a moment, and when it had cleared, El Capitan had vanished.

'You missed!' screamed Emmie-Lou.

'No.'

Herne had seen the arms fly up, and heard the clatter of stones as the bandit slid down the arroyo wall, landing in a tangle of limbs a few feet out from the bottom of the splintered rock.

'He's still alive.'

Herne put the gun down and walked unhurriedly across, unholstering the Colt as he went. He knew the shot had hit home, but it had been a difficult one, and he suspected the bullet might have missed the heart. El Capitan moved a little as he neared him, trying to lift his head to look at Jed.

There was blood across his chest on the left side. A lot of blood. It might not have been a direct kill, but Herne had seen enough bullet wounds to know that El Capitan wouldn't ever go raiding again.

'Senor Herne. I think you kill me. No?'

'Si. I think so.'

The naval cap was missing, and the face looked old and very tired, the eyes blinking vaguely around, scarcely able to focus on Herne. The Mexican was clearly puzzled by something.

'You came back . . . A man like you . . . For her . . . You came back . . . Why?'

'Man's got to live with himself.'

The head nodded, and then the eyes blanked and the body relaxed in the unmistakable last sleep of death. Emmie-Lou had joined Herne and she stood by his side, looking down at the body.

'What now?'

He turned to face her. 'Guess you know. I'm taking you home, Mrs. Parsons. Home.'

Chapter Fourteen

They took the high route back, riding the ridges and keeping clear of the valley trail. Nothing much happened, apart from seeing, several hundred feet below them, two Mexicans riding fast for the canyon, with leather bags slung across the pommels of their saddles.

'That's the half of the ransom. Ten thousand dollars. Why don't you take that and let me go. You'll finish a long way ahead.'

'Wrong. I'd finish a long way behind.'

'You're going to let them get away with it.'

'Like I said before, so I recollect, I got a contract with your husband and that's for two and a half thousand to bring you back. Nothing in the deal about any ten thousand dollars that I had to bring back as well.'

'My God, Jed Herne! You and my husband are both a couple of bastards.'

'Maybe. But in my case you could say that it was a happening at birth, while I hear your husband has worked real hard at it.'

The great black mausoleum still squatted blankly in the centre of a couple of hundred miles of nothing, its windows all shuttered. There was a small group of vaqueros and their women near the main door, and they parted silently and let Jed and the girl walk in, closing the door behind them.

Herne was in the house for less than five minutes, during which time Parsons said what he had to say, and Jed stopped him from saying more. The balance of the money was paid over and tucked firmly away. During all this, Emmie-Lou stood silent across the carved oak table in the dank gloom of the living-room. And said nothing.

'You will be leaving, Mister Herne?'

'Yeah. Got things to do. Can't say it's been a pleasure, but not much is.'

'You have done well. I could find a use for a man like you.'

'Guess I could find a use for you, Mister Parsons, but I figure I won't tell you what. So long, Mrs. Parsons.'

She ignored him, her finger tracing a pattern in the grey dust of the table. Her eyes only moved to look at the locked cupboard that Jed had seen inside on his last visit.

'I am grateful to you, and you have been paid for returning to me the leavings from the table of the Indians and the Mexicans. I assure you my wife will never cause anyone that kind of trouble again.'

'Why?'

'As long as she lives, she will never ever leave this house. Never.'

Herne the Hunter walked from the big mansion, breathing in the clean dry air of New Mexico, and the sun was shining. As the massive oak door swung shut, he thought he heard the rattling of chains and a scream. But it was probably only the bolts on the door clattering and squeaking.

Probably.

THE END

VIOLENCE AT SUNDOWN BY FRANK O'ROURKE

The town had been quiet for too long. Sooner or later there was bound to be violence in Olalla. A stray bullet and a dead cow-puncher were just the excuse two bitter men needed. The chance death gave them the reason to commit a vengeance killing . . . a reason to crush Marshal Bob Travis and the law he was pledged to uphold.

A tense Nebraska town splits wide open as a maddened range boss and his crafty foreman call the shots for VIOLENCE AT SUNDOWN.

0 552 10430 2 50p

LATIGO BY FRANK O'ROURKE

The idea was fool proof. Addis planned the action, Brotherton set the stage, and Ellington faked the holdup. They'd made the getaway at night after meeting at the river and splitting the haul. Then it would be lights out for the unsuspecting Ellington . . .

But they hadn't reckoned on the storm that flattened Ellington – and the money – and delivered both into the hands of Hester Johnson, who lived like a man, loved like a woman, and never forgot a grudge.

0 552 10407 8 50p

BELL OF DEATH BY LOUIS MASTERSON

Morgan Kane was cooling his heels in the forests of California with nothin' more pressing on his time than to catch himself a grizzly. But then he met up with a darn fool bunch of greenhorns on the trail of some long lost Aztec gold, and Kane's holiday turned into a deadly treasure hunt . . . a hunt that was shared by a savage band of escaped prisoners who'd shoot anyone who got in their way – child, woman, or U.S. Marshal . . .

0 552 10257 1 45P

THE DEMON FROM NICARAGUA BY LOUIS MASTERSON

Kane was a U.S. Marshal again. Six months after he'd thrown down his badge and quit, he was back – but only for a trial period. Old friends at Fort Leavenworth saw this was a new Kane: harsher and more brutal even than before – and they gave him just one chance to prove himself . . .

Kane hardly knew where Nicaragua was – some damn fool country in central America, he figured – but that was where they were sending him. And when he got there, he began to feel kinda easier in his mind: in that steamy country, he could smell death in the air . . .

0 552 10331 4 45P

SACKETT'S LAND BY LOUIS L'AMOUR

My first realization, after an immediate stab of fear, was that the Indians wore no paint. There were stories enough in England about Indians painting for war.

'Put your weapons out of sight', I said, 'below the gunwhales. I think they are peaceful.' The canoes slowed their pace, gliding down to us, and then a hand lifted, palm outward, and I recognized Potaka.

'It is my friend', I explained.

Rufisco snorted, 'No Indian is your friend,' he said, 'Keep your gun handy.'

0 552 09849 3 40p

THE CALIFORNIOS BY LOUIS L'AMOUR

Somewhere, in the mountains of California, there was gold. And the only man who knew where to find that gold was a strange old Indian, known as Juan . . .

The Mulkerins were Irish – a fierce, proud and independent family. But through a run of bad luck they found themselves in the debt of Zeke Wooston – a hard, cruel man who was just waiting to take their ranch if they didn't pay up. It looked as though the Mulkerins were going to have to fight Zeke's gang and the Law – until Sean Mulkerin remembered the story of the gold . . . If only they could find the gold, their troubles would be over . . . but first they had to find Juan – and time was running out – fast . . .

0 552 09696 2 35p